I0666922

ECHOES OF SMALL THINGS

ANNE M. BEGGS   ANA BRAZIL

EDIE CAY   C.V. LEE

JONATHAN POSNER

KATHRYN PRITCHETT

ALINA RUBIN

VANITHA SANKARAN

LINDA ULLESEIT

PAPER LANTERN WRITERS

This is a work of fiction. Names, characters, places, and incidents either are the product of the author's imagination or are used fictitiously and are not to be construed as real. Any resemblance to actual events, locales, organizations or persons, living or dead, is entirely coincidental.

Copyright © 2025 by Paper Lantern Writers

All rights reserved. No part of this book may be reproduced or used in any manner without written permission of the copyright owner except for the use of quotations in a book review. This book can not be used for training of artificial intelligence (AI). For more information, address: paperlanternwriters@gmail.com

First paperback edition November 2025

First digital edition November 2025

ISBN 979-8-9871222-9-7 (paperback)

ISBN 9798987122280 (ebook)

Published by Paper Lantern Writers

CONTENTS

SNIP, SNIP, SNIP   1
By Ana Brazil

THE RELUCTANT SAVIOR   17
By C.V. Lee

EIGHT   41
By Linda Ulleseit

THE STORM   69
By Anne M. Beggs

A NOT SO STILL LIFE, WITH APPLES   97
By Kathryn Pritchett

THE LADY RANGER OF YOSEMITE   109
By Edie Cay

THE SPIES' DILEMMA   141
Jonathan Posner

ABIGAIL'S NECKLACE   171
Alina Rubin

A HOUSE OF SALT   199
Vanitha Sankaran

Biographies   219
About Paper Lantern Writers   221
Also By Paper Lantern Writers   223

SNIP, SNIP, SNIP

BY ANA BRAZIL

In 1915, just after Easter, Private Paul Poiret came home on leave to Paris. Only months earlier, Private Poiret had been acknowledged as Paris's *King of Fashion*, and as such, he expected his return to be of great consequence. So far, however, it was not.

First, Poiret had been squashed into a third class carriage for the long train journey from Bordeaux. Then, when he finally arrived in Paris—hours before sunrise—it was raining. To add to his woes, he had no umbrella and could find no taxi. He arrived at his front door soaked from kepi to boot. He knocked and there was no answer. He had never needed a key to his house— his housekeeper and maids never seemed to sleep—and knowing that his cook *certainly* never left the kitchen, he trudged to the back of the house. After minutes of knocking, his wife answered the door.

His wife was surprised to see him, embracing him somewhat formally and without a kiss. She helped him from his great coat and then his smaller coat. He meant to go upstairs, to demand his bath and bed, but instead he collapsed on a chair at the small, square kitchen table. Once his wife removed his wet boots and double layer of socks, Poiret sat back almost contentedly, soaking up the warmth from the kitchen stove.

It was minutes before Poiret realized there was no cook to serve him coffee, boil his eggs, or bring him pastries. Instead, his wife busied herself about the stove.

He attempted to engage her—*I have had a headache since yesterday; I need a new umbrella*—but instead of replying, she kept to her kitchen duties. As his wife ignored him, he wondered if he should have kept in touch with his mistress, whom he had last seen when he was mobilized eight months ago. His mistress always greeted him enthusiastically when he arrived, and *she* was always eager for his company. Even more importantly, *she* was always a marvel to behold: her deep eyes lined with kohl, her round lips painted, and her body bedecked in the colorful, luxurious, and fanciful Orient-influenced garments created by Poiret at his now-shuttered *Maison du Poiret*.

Poiret's wife, to his bewilderment, had bunched her hair into a bun and wore no makeup. Even worse was her drab brown dress, which hung straight, like two long potato sacks sewn together. Perhaps the fabric was linen, although it was rough and burly like burlap. The garment had no trim, no embroidery, no buttons, and no embellishment of any kind. And were those really pockets sewn into the side seams?

The brown dress was slightly fitted to her form, but it was not tight enough, and there was nothing sensual about it: neither her breasts nor her buttocks were defined. The saggy dress was better suited for a woman who swept floors at the market or rooted out rats from basements. *Not* the wife of Paris's premiere couturier.

Yet, despite the awkwardness, the ugliness of the garment, he saw something... *workable*? in the design. This revelation made the drab dress even worse, for had it been intentionally created? Worse still, how could his wife—who had been his muse and model, exulting in beautiful clothes, hairdressings, and cosmetics—*choose* to wear it?

His wife served him coffee in a kitchen mug and took a half loaf of bread from the cupboard. With the warmth of the kitchen, his coffee steaming in front of him, and a Gitane between his fingers, Poiret might have finally relaxed.

Except for that one small thing that would not allow him to relax.

"*Merde*," he reflected as he lit his cigarette. "That damn coat."

When his wife did not stop what she was doing to look at him, he raised his voice. "I was informed before going on leave... the Army is no longer producing my new coat."

As his wife slipped a folded knife from her pocket and set the half baguette of bread on a board, Poiret recounted his sad story.

"My redesign of the Army great coat—a relic from the 1870s!—was an inspiration. I made one small change— changing the double-breast into a single-breast—and saved the army sixty centimeters of wool per coat. Sixty! I worked a miracle for the Army. For France."

Poiret expected some agreement from his wife, but instead, she focused on slicing the baguette with the short blade of her pocketknife. Poiret watched long enough to know that she was slicing the bread all wrong, and he quickly corrected her. "*Non.* Never saw the blade back and forth; you must put the knife atop the bread and force it through."

Pleased at his correction, Poiret sat back in his chair. His still steaming mug of coffee reminded him of his last steaming Turkish bath, and he relaxed even deeper into his chair and completed his own thoughts.

"But now, the higher-ups are saying that my coat wasn't warm enough during the winter. That the single-breast did not cover the soldiers as well as the double-breast. That my coats are responsible for the soldiers catching pneumonia! I'm getting blamed for the death of every soldier who died this winter."

Poiret removed the saucer from beneath his mug and stubbed his cigarette onto it. *Merde!*

And it never would have happened, he never would have been blamed for hundreds of soldiers catching and dying from pneumonia while wearing his new coat, if Archduke Ferdinand's stupid, stupid, chauffeur had not taken a wrong turn in Sarajevo and driven his carriage straight to an anarchist with a gun.

Such a small thing, that wrong turn, yet it launched the war. A war that ruined Poiret's reign in French couture and, after being posted to the Army's Tailoring Regiment, led him to design a single-breasted Army coat.

Poiret blew on his coffee and sipped, surprised by the unexpected flavor of calvados. The apple brandy quickly warmed him through and through. He gulped his café calva greedily, and the worries of the war seemed to recede. Finally relaxed, Poiret sat back in his chair and looked at his wife.

For the first time, he realized that the drab brown dress she wore was hemmed midway between her knees and ankles. Although Poiret had also experimented with shortened hems, he had never designed a hem so short, so immodest. And yet, Poiret liked what he saw.

Those ankles. Poiret sipped from the kitchen mug again. His wife's slender yet muscular ankles had always excited him, and today, assisted by the delicious café calva, they excited him even more. He ignored her present drab appearance and remembered his wife in her glory before the war, as she modeled his famous hobble skirt for him.

If he could see her in that skirt again, if he could watch as she took tiny, feminine steps away from him. Watch as her legs flexed under the heavy silk, as her thighs rolled ever so slowly, as her sumptuous derriere strained against the material, begging for his hands to cradle and squeeze them.

He imagined going to her right now, standing behind her and putting the palms of his hands under her derriere. But the sudden heaviness of fatigue kept him in his chair.

Still, unable to let go, he asked, "Do you, do you still have *that skirt*?"

He did not have to specify that hobble skirt, of course, because there had been only one skirt that had ever excited him. Only one skirt ever that had been directly responsible for the births of two of their four children.

"*That skirt?*" he asked again, now annoyed at her silence.

He flattened his hands on the table, forcing himself up from the chair. Her long silence this morning, just like her silences through the years, had been irksome. He wanted a response from her, and he would get it. But before he could reach her, she turned around, a plate of sliced bread in one hand, her open pocketknife in the other, the blade set toward him.

"*Non*," his wife replied. "When we ran out of wood," her eyes went to the stove, "that skirt was the first thing I burned."

Madame Denise Poiret, after watching her husband stuff his mouth with toast and gulp another café calva, assisted him to his bed. She had sacrificed her last quarter bottle of apple calvados to his coffee mug, and with luck he might sleep the entire day. She left the house minutes after his first snore.

Although the rain had cleared for the moment, dark clouds lingered above. Yet Denise's thoughts were darker, because she was overwhelmed with memories of *that skirt*.

Poiret had been inspired to create that skirt during a trip to the racetrack, where he'd been fascinated by a mare with her two front legs tied together. The mare could not move, no matter how hard she struggled against the hobbling. For some God-awful reason, Poiret immediately dragged Denise to his work-room. Over several hours he sewed a very narrow skirt onto her. Not only did the skirt hug her from derriere to ankles, hobbling her just as much as the mare had been hobbled, but Poiret also crisscrossed two ribbons inside the bottom of the skirt to further imprison her ankles.

Denise hated the skirt instantly. Poiret was just as instantly aroused and demanded that she model it throughout Paris. Unable to walk even a few inches at a time, Denise had often been forced to use a walking stick to keep from falling down. And yet weeks later, Denise and gullible, fashionable Parisiennes squeezed themselves into Poiret's hobble skirt, cementing his reputation as the *King of Fashion*.

So, it was a brief moment of triumph this morning, to tell Poiret that she had burned that skirt, even though her brave words were a lie.

Courage, she reminded herself. *You knew he would return some day and find out what you've been up to. You also knew that he would not like it.* Denise had expected a reckoning with Poiret eventually, *oui,* but she had not expected it to be so soon.

Unlike so many other wives in Paris, Denise had not been eager for her husband's return. Despite the food and fuel short-ages that daunted Paris, her lack of household help, and even her children's night terrors, Madame Denise Poiret was extremely happy to be a woman on her own.

She especially did not miss Poiret and his demands. After nine years of marriage, no longer did her husband tell her what to do, how to do it, and what to wear every hour of the day. With Poiret's voice silenced, Denise could finally hear her own thoughts. And she'd been very surprised to realize that all her thoughts were about...how she had nothing to wear.

Oui, before the war her husband had designed closets of clothing for her. She had morning, afternoon, dinner, and evening dresses, and fête and racetrack and Deauville dresses galore, all appropriate for her leisurely life before the war. But now, as she ran her own home, cooked her children's meals, and volunteered for zeppelin-spotting duty, she realized that all her dresses were inadequate. What she—and the women working amongst the refugees, assisting doctors in hospitals, and keeping their husbands' shops open—needed was a dress suitable for a Parisienne at war.

And so, Denise set out to make one.

She knew exactly what she needed: a dress that did not bind, slow, or hamper her. A dress with a hem that would not catch on the tram steps; a dress with man-sized pockets; a dress that did not show soiling easily. A dress that allowed ease of movement but did not require too much material, because fabric was *très cher* these days.

Denise set up shop at the shuttered-but-still-under-lease *Maison du Poiret* at 9 Avenue d'Antin, and today, she let herself inside the maison through the back door. She entered into the well-organized workroom, not completely surprised to see Cécile, Poiret's former *premiere* and now hers, on her knees, removing a pin from the hem of a mannequin's dress. Denise froze in place, respectful of Cécile's concentration. The mannequin, a girl named Flore who had been well-trained to not move, offered Denise a weak smile.

The dress Flore wore was the final version of the dress Denise wore today; a dress Denise had easily thrown over her head and fastened without assistance. Denise had worn her dress for days to understand the good and bad about it and had made careful decisions on how to improve it. One thing she did not change were the enormous, reinforced pockets on each side seam; pockets that enabled her to keep her pocketknife, scissors, handkerchief, and coin purse with her at all times.

Cécile cocked her head one way and then another. She nodded, rose to her feet, and joined Denise. No words of greeting were needed between the two women, because before they had been dressmaker and *premiere*, they had been friends.

It was on the tip of Denise's tongue, to share with Cécile that Poiret had returned, but as she gazed at Flore, as she realized the triumph of her dress, she did not want to spoil the moment. Denise stifled a yawn, wishing she had not used her last tablespoons of coffee grounds on Poiret's café calva.

"The linen is a very good choice," said Cécile. "As is the sable brown color. It is especially attractive in the sunlight, you know."

Cécile herself was wearing black in honor of her fallen brother, and once again Denise wondered at the wisdom of offering a brown dress when so many women were engulfed in multiple layers of black. The quick victory against Germany had not happened, might not happen soon, and there was no telling when women would stop wearing black.

"I have always loved linen," Denise replied. "So soft. So generous. So easy to move in. We were fortunate to find those bolts in the backroom, although I can't imagine what they were purchased for."

Cécile nodded and then commanded Flore to turn full circle.

Despite standing on a two-foot high plinth, Flore easily turned to her right. The dress did not stifle her movement; did not trip her up.

Flore turned full circle again, to her left.

"Raise your arms, petite," instructed Cécile. "Higher, toward the sky."

Flore performed as requested, the brown linen dress moving with her.

Reminded suddenly of her youngest daughter, Denise said, "Touch your toes and then your nose."

Flore did as Denise asked, and it was then that Denise saw a hanging thread. She approached Flore, removed a sheathed scissors from her voluminous pocket, and snipped a half inch of thread from a seam.

Denise joined her friend once more. "I did not know until I started working with you, Cécile, how the smallest change can make the most difference to a garment."

Cécile looked directly at Denise, as if hearing her hesitation. "There's something else you would change about this dress?"

Denise wavered slightly, indecision settling about her like a mantle. Yet, she and Cécile had discussed this, that when designing a dress, it was the attention to details—the size of a button or the length of a stitch or the angle of a dart—that mattered most.

"Oui," Denise slowly circled around the mannequin. She looked down at the hem of her own dress. Her mid-calf hem was useful, but still, it restricted her. "We need to shorten the hem."

"But I've already—"

"A shorter dress allows for more movement, more freedom. If we have to take over men's jobs, we need the same freedoms a man has. Just think what you and I could have accomplished years ago if our dresses had been shorter and looser. Think of what our daughters can do now." Denise thought briefly of her daughters, who, like her husband, she left sleeping. "And by my calculations, if we raise the hem eight inches above the ankle, we will save a quarter yard of material for each dress."

Denise was ready to take her scissors to the hem and make the alteration herself, but she refrained, respecting Cécile's authority as premiere.

Cécile nodded in agreement. "And with an easy pattern like this, our seamstresses will save hours in sewing." Cécile pulled the fabric measuring tape from around her neck and looked at it. "I will remove another four inches from the dress. Is that all, then?"

Denise took a minute to enjoy her decision, and then, shared her news. "Poiret returned home."

She was gratified to hear her friend gasp.

"At four this morning," Denise continued. "For twenty-four hour leave." Then, "He looked dead on his feet when he arrived and drank two mugs of café calva before going to bed."

Cécile tensed. "Does he know what we've been doing?"

"Non," Denise replied. "He knows nothing. He didn't even ask about the children."

Then, as Flore released a huge yawn, Denise asked, "Have you two been here all night?"

"I suppose we have," replied Cécile. She looked out the window onto the workshop's backstreet. The rain had returned. "But—"

"Go," Denise yawned as if she'd caught Cécile and Flore's fatigue. "Go home and rest. I will finish up here."

Cécile nodded her agreement to Flore and the mannequin stepped down easily from the plinth. She stretched her arms high above her head, and bent this way and that, this time for her own pleasure. Flore walked towards the door leading to the mannequin's dressing room and both Denise and Cécile watched the girl, satisfied that their design could be useful to so many women.

"*Bon*," they said at the same time.

Cécile followed after Flore, and Denise sat in her spot at the room's largest cutting table. She retrieved her latest designs from the cutting table drawer and spread them in front of her. The brown linen dress was what women needed right now, but was it possible they might need something else in the future? Could the war necessitate more changes to how they dressed?

Lulled by the rhythm of the rain upon the workroom window, Denise slipped forward and laid her arms on the table. She cradled her head in the crook of her elbow, not caring that she slipped from reverie into slumber.

"Mon Dieu!" Poiret's voice blared like a fireman's trumpet announcing a zeppelin attack.

Denise awoke suddenly, startled first by Poiret's shrillness and then the realization that she'd fallen asleep at the worktable.

"What have you done to my workshop?" Poiret continued his assault. "What are you even doing here? This was all closed when I left Paris and was supposed to stay closed."

Denise blinked, slowly lifting her head from her arms and sitting up on the stool, all the while attempting to focus her thoughts. Poiret stood in the middle of the workroom, dressed in his uniform, his kepi still perched upon his head.

Poiret's gaze searched through the workroom—*her* workroom now—and he took in the rolls of fabrics on the shelves; Celine's basket of pins, needles, and scissors on the cutting table; the two sewing machines set against the windowed wall, and the sketches of dresses and blouses and bonnets scattered in front of her.

Finally, Poiret's eyes focused on a wire mannequin positioned on the same plinth that Flore had been standing on earlier. The mannequin was wearing Flore's brown linen dress, and Denise realized that Cécile must have cut off four inches, hemmed the dress, and put it on the mannequin as she slept.

The rain had stopped, and the sun returned, giving the

brown linen a rich, almost-golden sheen. It was glorious, Denise's creation. Just a few small changes to two yards of left-over linen, and the women of Paris could trade their fussy and impractical garments for a comfortable and utilitarian dress.

Denise could not resist a smile. A few weeks ago, she had only an *idea*. Today, she had a *dress*. But as Denise admired her lovely creation, Poiret's brow creased, and his face flushed. His words, low and steady, resonated through the workroom.

"What is this abomination?"

Denise braced her hands on the table, her sketches lined up before her like soldiers at her defense. She took a breath before replying.

"It's a dress I designed to serve the women of Paris."

Poiret stopped to take his own breath. "Designed for the laundress? A dress so ugly she must hide it under her apron?"

Denise gazed once more at her dress. It was not ugly, but she did see another loose thread, this time from one of the pockets. One snip of her scissors and the dress would be perfect.

Poiret's face reddened further, as it did when he wanted to argue. "Maybe a dress for the rat catchers at the Opera House?"

"It's a dress for a teacher, so she may move around the class-room, assisting her students. Or for a ticket taker on the tram, so she can walk up the stairs without tripping. Or—"

Denise stopped herself, knowing her husband would never listen to her. She changed her tack. "Parisiennes have changed since you've been gone. We are all working now."

"Bah! Parisiennes will never change. They will always want luxury. They will always want opulence, ornament. They will always want a Paul Poiret original."

"You have no idea how much women have changed during the war. Or what women want to wear. *Your* clothes are not fit for the war. They belong to another time and place." *How true,* Denise realized suddenly. "Your clothes have been cast into the back of closets. They are not worn now, and they will never be worn again."

"Yes," Poiret peered at his wife, not the least flustered by her vigor. "I know something about clothing at the back of closets."

Denise, who had been gazing at the stray thread on the brown linen dress, slowly looked at Poiret. Their eyes locked and second by second, Denise's confidence crumbled. *He knew.*

Poiret removed his leather gloves, undid one button of his coat, and stuffed a hand inside. Slowly, he pulled out *that skirt*, which had been rolled into a purple silk cylinder. He shook it out like he was unfurling a flag.

"Look what I found at the back of your own closet! How dare you tell me that you burned this skirt!"

Denise stared at the hated skirt, angered that some sense of wifely loyalty had made her hide it instead of slashing open the seams and ripping the hobble mechanism from the ankles. Her hand against her pocket, she felt the scissors inside. With anger pumping through her body, Denise Poiret decided that today would be the day. Today she would destroy the skirt.

Poiret tossed the skirt across his shoulder, headed to the wire mannequin, and began tearing at the brown linen dress. Denise watched him, horrified and unable to move as he ripped at the neck and pulled at the pockets. Poiret knew exactly where to attack the dress and he quickly tore it from the mannequin and tossed it to the ground.

He slipped the purple skirt over the top of the wire mannequin, caressing the silk over the narrow shoulders. With the skirt at the waist, he buttoned the waistband and released the skirt. It fell to a few inches above the top of the plinth.

As Poiret adjusted the skirt around the mannequin, Denise remembered each of the eighteen small buttons set into the back and how Poiret had positioned them so that she could not unbutton them herself.

Poiret stepped back to admire his creation. "Delicious. Even with the wrinkles. Now tell me, which would a Parisienne prefer to wear? This..." he looked lovingly at the skirt, "Or those brown rags on the floor?"

Although Denise seemed fixed to her stool, her voice did not desert her. "*My dress* may look like nothing to you, but for the women of Paris, being able to move our arms and waists and thighs and legs means everything. And it could mean everything to France."

To her surprise, Denise found that she was clutching the scissors in her hand. She quickly unsheathed them. The scissors were small, but solid, strong, and cold, and she was buoyed by their presence. With the remnants of her beautiful brown linen dress on the floor, she knew what she must do. She pushed back her stool and stood. Then held her scissors just as she'd held her knife in the kitchen. This time she aimed at *that skirt*.

Poiret froze for only a second, then he started toward his wife, his entire body alert and prepared to stop her.

Denise raised the scissors high above her head, like a butcher with a cleaver.

"Stop right there," she warned.

But Poiret did not stop. Instead, he launched at her, grabbing at the scissors in her hand.

"Let go," he commanded, as if speaking to a mongrel dog guarding a bone.

Denise held fast to the scissors, fighting Poiret for their possession. He pulled; she pulled back. He twisted; she twisted back. She had not thought it possible, but she held her own as they struggled. *He's gotten softer during the war*, she thought, *while I have gotten stronger*.

Yet just as Denise tugged with the entire might of her new strength, Poiret tugged harder, and the scissors were his.

Denise grabbed at them, capturing the tapered inches of the

blade. They were narrow and slippery, but she would not let go. Face to face, breath to breath, wife and husband struggled in fury until Denise heard the scissors tinkle to the floor. With a quick sweep of her right foot, she kicked the scissors away, hearing them slide far across the floor.

Reveling in the freedom that her new dress gave her, Denise brought her knee up to Poiret's groin—something she could never do in *that skirt*—but he backed up just in time. They stared at each for seconds, until he turned toward the fallen scissors, as if to reclaim them. Without hesitation, Denise threw herself at Poiret, pushing him with all her strength. He stumbled backwards, tripped, and collapsed to the floor, his fall cushioned by the mound of brown linen.

Denise expected him to rise and come at her again. Instead, he looked at her, as if waiting for her to assist him. When she did not, he slid further into the shredded linen.

With Poiret subdued, Denise gave her full attention to the purple silk skirt, appraising it like the true enemy it was. It was tight. It was physically dangerous. It was evil.

She looked over to her small scissors across the floor. Good friend that it was, she needed a stronger ally. She opened a drawer in the cutting table. Inside were six large, sharp scissors, and she chose the largest pair.

Fully expecting that Poiret was watching her, Denise opened and closed the scissors, reveling in their crisp *snip, snip, snip*. They were as sharp as they were large. *Oui*, they would do the job.

Author's Note

In this story I wanted to pay homage to that moment during World War I when someone in France realized that for a woman to *get the job done*, she needed a multi-pocketed, mid-calf length, loose dress. The type of dress, it has been argued, that liberated women from constricting clothing *forever*. Although we all know that the new French dress was quickly adopted around the world—and continued as the fashionable silhouette for women until the end of the 1920's—who could have guessed that the small decision to shorten a dress hem would launch a women's clothing revolution?

History does not record who created that first dress, but I've long imagined that Denise Poiret—the ever-suffering wife of *King of Fashion* Paul Poiret—wielded her scissors in the design.

THE RELUCTANT SAVIOR

BY C.V. LEE

Isle of Jersey
Mid-October, 1483

Clement Le Hardy trudged across the rain-pocked sand, his cloak billowing and snapping with each gust of wind. The waves slammed against the shore; for days, the storm had churned the waters of Grouville Bay. He hunched his shoulders and pressed on. He would rather be anywhere but here—only he had nowhere else to go.

His wife, Wilhelmina, was heavy with child and easily vexed. He could endure her presence no longer, but casting her out into the downpour would incur unwelcome judgment. Thus, he must be the one to leave.

Ahead, Mont Orgueil loomed high on the rocks, the castle glowing like a beacon in the storm. He ground his teeth. Governor Harleston—the selfish dastard who dismissed his every petition—had made his home there.

"Be content," Harleston said, as though Clement's paltry life was fair compensation for all he had lost. He had been born for greater things, and one day he would reclaim what was rightfully his—the dignity of his birthright. Just how he would accomplish it escaped him.

In the distance, two ships pitched and rocked in the turbulent waters as they sailed southward. Clement shook his head. No one in their sound mind would leave safe harbor in this weather. Dullards. The world was full of them. He wondered idly which of the two ships would capsize first.

A dark shape bobbed in the waves. As it drifted closer, a faint cry sounded above the roar of the wind. Clement stopped and stared, blinked, and stared again. Was that a man being swept along with the tide?

The man must have washed overboard and now was struggling to keep from drowning. He had made his choice and would have to live—or die—with the consequences. People had often told Clement the same: to accept his fate, even though he was the victim of choices not his own.

Clement continued northward, battling the blustery wind and pelting rain, pretending he had neither seen nor heard the desperate man. Served the doddypoll right for putting his life in danger. Besides, Clement had a wife and two boys at home with a babe on the way. What would become of them if he lost his life trying to be a hero?

A hero! Clement stopped short. Perhaps if he performed this selfless deed, he would gain the governor's favor. His bravery would be lauded for years to come by the isle folk. Maybe this would be the very thing that would convince Governor Harleston to plead Clement's case before King Richard.

He unfastened his cloak and carefully folded it. Pulling off his boots, he set them atop, then removed his woolen stockings and stuffed them inside.

Fortunately, the man was now nearer the shore, thus reducing the risk. Clement took a deep breath and plunged in. His lungs seized as he hit the icy water, and he struggled to catch his breath. Taking long strokes, he battled the powerful waves that sought to deposit him back on the shore. As he neared the stranger, the man sank beneath the waves. Clement dived down, clutching a handful of the man's tunic. As they broke the surface, they both gasped for air.

Already his limbs felt weak, his legs cramping in the freezing water. As he rested, the waves buffeted them about, filling his mouth with salty water. He began the short, but difficult, swim back to land. His strength flagged with each stroke; the weight and drag of the flailing man hampered his forward motion. If the man panicked and fought him, this act of magnanimity would prove the death of them both. He stopped again to rest, struggling to keep them both afloat.

With the shore now so close, he continued. When they reached shallow water, he helped the man stand, wrapping one of the man's arms about his neck. As the furious waves crashed against the strand, the man stumbled, threatening to pull Clement down with him, but Clement managed to keep upright. When they reached the shore, they collapsed on the sand, shivering, teeth chattering.

The two men sat side by side in silence for several minutes, panting as they tried to catch their breath.

The man brushed his thin, lank hair from his face and coughed up a bit of water. Clement recoiled at the man's long face and sharp nose. *Had I known his countenance to be so revolting, I would have let him drown.* Although younger than Clement's thirty-seven years, the man was probably an unfortunate nobody, a lowly seaman trying to make a living. But now that Clement had made the rescue, he would extract any advantage this act of valor might bring.

"How can I ever thank you?" The man was well-spoken, although Clement could not place his accent—neither purely English nor French.

"Just doing my Christian duty." Clement scrambled up and retrieved his cloak and boots.

"Well, whatever the reason, I am obliged to you," the man replied.

Clement brushed the sand from his feet and pulled on his sodden stockings and boots. "My name is Clement Le Hardy. And you are?"

The man stared blankly before responding. "Simon."

Clement fastened on his cloak, then reached his hand out to the stranger. "Pleased to meet you, Simon. Let me take you to my humble home where you can get dry and fed."

Simon's eyes darted from side-to-side like a trapped animal seeking a route of escape. "I have imposed enough already."

How insolent of this man to refuse his proffered hand. Nevertheless, Clement opted to play the Good Samaritan. "Nonsense. After saving you from drowning, I could not leave you here to die of cold."

"Your thoughtfulness does you credit, but I must decline," Simon replied. "I need to get back to my boat."

"What boat? I saw no boat, only two ships in the distance."

Simon stared out across the water, saying nothing.

"Why were you out in this storm?" Clement asked.

"Fishing," the stranger replied, still breathing heavily after his ordeal.

Clement looked askance. "I suspect the storm has broken up your vessel by now. Whatever possessed you to go out in this weather?"

Lightning flashed over the water and thunder rumbled. "It is not like I planned to encounter a storm," Simon replied.

Given the storm had been raging for several days, the man's explanation was suspect. But now was not the time for questions. Clement waved the offered hand. "Come! Let us not delay any longer. It is dangerous out here. We must seek shelter."

Simon shook his head. "I do not wish to appear ungrateful, but no one must know I am here."

Grasping Simon's hand, Clement pulled him up. "Why?"

Simon pulled away from Clement and sat back down in the wet sand, grabbing a handful and squishing it through his fingers. "Suffice it to say the consequences will be grave if the wrong people learn of my presence. I must return to Brittany forthwith."

"And how do you propose to get there? Swim?" Clement shook his head. The man must be mad, although he did not seem so. "I assure you, I know not who you are, and I doubt anyone on this miserable isle does. Hence, there is no reason to tempt death."

When Simon looked away and did not respond, Clement strode off, then yelled over his shoulder, "What a fine display of gratitude! I risked my life to save yours—now you are just going to throw it away? Had I known, I would have left you to drown."

"When you put it that way—" Simon rose, the water dripped from his clothes onto the sand as he hastened to catch up to Clement. "Do you mind lending me your hat?"

"Have I not done enough for you already?" Clement felt his ire rising. "On account of your foolishness, I may spend the next week abed. Now you demand my hat."

Simon did not blink. "Yes, I do," he said firmly, as if he expected unquestioning obedience.

Clement quickened his step.

"Where are you taking me?" Simon asked, his voice higher-pitched than before.

Clearly something was amiss with this man, but Clement determined to humor him until the mystery was solved. "You may shelter in my stable. I shall send my groom home until I figure out what to do with you."

Simon looked up at the thickly clouded sky. "Hopefully, this storm will soon pass."

Clement pointed to the small copse beyond the manor house, some three hundred paces from the stable. "Hide among the trees," he said. "I will signal when it is safe."

Simon put out his hand. "Your hat."

Grudgingly, Clement removed the sodden cap and handed it to him. Simon snatched it and pulled it low over his forehead, then lurched toward the trees, disappearing within.

Clement hastened to the stable and slid open the door. The horse snorted and shuffled about his stall. The ass brayed—such a hideous noise. He would kill the nasty beast, but it had belonged to his dearly departed uncle, and he had vowed to keep the animal until all that had been stolen from him was restored.

The groom rushed forward and bowed. "Seigneur Le Hardy, do you require your horse?"

"Not today."

"You are soaked. Is something wrong?"

"Nay, I got caught in the downpour."

The groom's brow furrowed, and, given the downpour had continued for several days, Clement realized his explanation was as illogical as Simon's. "Take a few days respite with your family. I will see to the horse and the ass."

"'Tis most generous." The groom bowed again. "*Gramercy*, Seigneur."

The groom collected his meager belongings and hurried out into the rain. Clement watched as the groom scurried down the pathway toward his home. When he disappeared from sight, Clement gestured to Simon, who bounded out of the trees and raced across the green, water splashing up with each step. Once inside, he shook his head, droplets spattering in all directions.

"I shall return shortly with food, blankets, and dry clothes," Clement said.

Simon settled onto a pile of hay and peeled off his boots and stockings. "I will be here, for I have nowhere to go."

Clement held out his hand. "My hat. Should I return without it, it would raise suspicion."

Removing the hat, Simon handed it back, and Clement clapped it onto his head.

He stepped out of the stable, slid the door shut, and barred it. Not that he really expected Simon—or whatever his real name was—would go anywhere, but he did not want to take any chances. He stood beneath the thatched overhang, watching the rain pour down in sheets, awaiting a break.

Simon was quite peculiar, and clearly hiding a secret. Perhaps he was an escaped criminal. *Fie! What have I gotten myself into?*

The rain lulled, and Clement strode toward the manor house, careful to avoid the large puddles that had formed.

A servant opened the door and bowed. "Pleased you are home safe, Seigneur Le Hardy."

Clement pulled the sodden hat from his head and dropped it on the floor. "Only for a few brief moments. I must return to the stable. See that the cook provides me with an ample supply of food." Clement turned his back so the servant could remove his cloak. "I will need several blankets and do not wish to be disturbed."

Cloak in hand, the servant bowed, his eye twitching. "Yes, seigneur." He knelt and retrieved the hat as Clement crossed the great hall.

Clement climbed the stairs to the lord's chamber. Wilhelmina lay asleep on the bed, her face peaceful. Unforgivable, after she made his life so miserable. It was more than her volatile behavior that irked him. After losing his inheritance, he must attribute his improved standing in society to her inheritance of Astelle Manor. A fact that was a constant source of humiliation.

Grumbling, he peeled off his wet clothes. Hopefully, his ill-advised foray into the raging waters did not entirely ruin them. He stepped to the hearth, seeking to warm his body. He would take Simon food and supplies when the rain subsided. After all, why risk another drenching? The man had shown only a modicum of gratitude when he owed his life to Clement.

A groggy voice asked, "Clement, is that you?" Wilhelmina sat up, her blond tresses falling about her shoulders. "Where have you been?"

She was a beautiful woman, although his resentment rendered her less attractive. But she was still a female body to warm his bed at night, or during the day, if the mood struck. "I went for a walk, *ma chérie*," Clement replied.

Her eyes widened. "You must be chilled." She patted his empty place on the bed. "Come, let me warm you."

He crossed to the wardrobe and selected dry garments. "Another time. I have urgent business to attend."

"In this storm?" Her lower lip protruded. "Can the servants not handle it?"

"Unfortunately, no," he said as he pulled on a clean pair of hose and adjusted the codpiece. "It is a matter of some delicacy. I may not be home tonight."

She rose, padded over to him, and placed a kiss on his cheek. "But I need you here with me," she whined, placing a hand on his chest.

Clement pulled away and presented his back as he laced up his doublet and strapped on a girdle.

"I pray you do not intend to sleep outside in the storm."

He rolled his eyes. "Must you always be so dramatic? I am a grown man and do not need your mothering."

"My apologies, Seigneur. I did not mean to cause offence."

Her voice was hushed, and he knew she made that annoying penitent face.

"I will let you make it up to me."

"Anything, Clement."

"Should anyone ask about my absence at supper tonight, be prepared with some excuse."

"As you wish," she whispered.

He pulled on his old, scuffed boots. Rummaging through the dresser, he found a dagger and slipped it into his girdle. After assembling an additional set of clothes, he quit the room.

The wind and rain quietened, and he vacated the house, stopping by the cookhouse to collect the basket of food and the blankets. He checked the contents and had the cook add three more flasks of ale. Simon might need some encouragement to speak freely.

Although it was awkward trying to juggle everything without the help of a servant, Clement made it to the stable with nary a mishap. He drew back the latch and slid the stable door open.

"Simon," he whispered loudly. "It is I, Clement."

Simon peeked around the corner of the furthermost stall before coming out into the open.

"I brought victuals, blankets, and dry clothes." Clement set them on the ground. "Why were you hiding?"

"I was unsure if I could trust you. I feared you might return with the constable," Simon said.

"Why would I do that?" Clement handed Simon a blanket and the dry clothes. "You have given me no cause to think that is necessary."

Taking the garments and the blanket, Simon ducked out of sight. Clement searched for a flint and lantern, hung it high so the stable was flooded with light, then slid the door closed again. He opened the basket, withdrew a small cloth, and spread it on the ground. Then came two tankards, followed by a variety of cold meats, cheeses, and bread. All he needed now was to get a couple of tankards of ale into the man to loosen his tongue.

Simon returned wearing the dry clothes, the blanket draped over his shoulders, and settled onto the ground across from Clement. He eyed the food hungrily. Clement poured a hearty portion of ale and handed the tankard to Simon. "Drink up. It will warm your blood."

Clement withdrew two trenchers and piled each high with food. "Not much of a feast, but there is plenty for both of us."

Simon picked up a portion of eel with his pale, smooth hands, and placed it on his tongue.

Clement shuddered, disgusted by Simon's yellowish-brown teeth. He swallowed hard, determined not to let his revulsion keep him from uncovering the truth. "How long have you been a fisher?"

The man blinked rapidly, but he quickly schooled his countenance. "Well—I—F-f-for nigh a decade now. I was apprenticed at a young age."

Simon's visage showed none of the weathered look of a fisher. Ten years of sun and wind would leave their mark on any man, but Simon's skin was smooth and scarcely tanned. The man clearly did not trust Clement with the smallest bit of information about himself.

"And where do you hail from?" Clement asked as he sliced off a healthy portion of cheese and handed it to his guest.

"I grew up in Wales, but have lived in Brittany for many years." Simon took a long draught of ale, eyeing Clement with great interest.

That explained the man's unusual accent. The fact that Simon, or whatever his real name was, feared someone on the isle would recognize him meant he must be a personage of some importance. On Jersey, no one would know a commoner from

Wales or Brittany. Unless... The puzzle pieces were falling into place. Perchance a traitor, a supporter of Henry Tudor—which presented interesting possibilities.

If Simon was indeed a man of consequence, Clement knew he must make the most of it. When an opportunity presented itself, only a fool would not seek some personal gain. Money was always scarce at Astelle Manor, and a bit of coin would tide them through until the next harvest.

The Fates had surely smiled upon him this day, putting in his custody not just a prisoner, for he had locked the man in his stable, but in all probability a traitor. It only stood to reason that a handsome reward would be paid for handing over such a one to the crown.

The corner of his mouth ticked as he thought about the honor it would bring him if he turned over a man guilty of treason.

"Can I depend on you and your discretion to get me home?" Simon asked.

"You ask much of me without telling me who you are, particularly if helping you might land me in trouble. Pray tell, are you an escaped criminal? Or a traitor to the crown? Not that I would blame you. King Richard is a despicable man."

"I am no criminal, but you are well informed." Simon took another long draught. "No one wishes to fall into the hands of that king."

Clement sighed. "I fear we are stuck with him now his nephews have mysteriously vanished."

Simon shook his head, his face sorrowful. "A pity, indeed. Although I hear rumors that many are throwing their allegiance behind Henry Tudor. Even the Duke of Buckingham, King Richard's staunchest supporter, has turned against him."

"If only!" Clement replied. "But I think that is a far cry from coming to pass." He stared at Simon. "How came you to live in Brittany?"

"My family supported the House of Lancaster. My mother sent me away to live in Brittany after King Edward ascended the throne. I was young, so I remember very little."

"Consider yourself lucky. My life was good during King Henry's reign. My family suffered much under King Edward." Clement lifted the flask and refilled Simon's tankard before continuing. It seemed to be having the desired effect. "If only the Lancastrians were back on the throne."

The man stared at Clement. "Treasonous words. I hope you are not expressing those sentiments openly."

Perhaps he had misjudged the man, but he would press the point further. Given the man's desire to keep his presence here secret, he doubted Simon would betray him.

"Certainly, it is not a popular opinion on the isle. People love Governor Harleston, but I see him for the opportunist he is. He is good to those he deems worthy—mostly his son-in-law—but for people like me... He has made every effort to keep me in my diminished station."

"Sounds like you have quite a story," Simon replied, taking another draught.

Clement watched him closely. "I will not deign to bore you with the details. Many years have passed since. I am resigned to my fate. Besides, you have no power to change it." Tearing off two hunks of bread, he handed one to Simon. "You mentioned two things that have me thinking. House of Lancaster and Brittany. Have you made the acquaintance of Henry Tudor?"

"Unfortunately, no. Why do you ask?"

"Only that I have huge respect for his mother," Clement said. "Although I have not had the privilege of meeting Lady Margaret Beaufort, nor anyone else of import in England, I hear rumors she advocates for her son, desiring that one day he may be king." He took a bite of bread and chewed thoughtfully. "How King Richard allows her to keep her head, I cannot imagine."

"I can only surmise," Simon replied.

Clement lifted the flask. "We have all night, and plenty of ale. Let us spend it telling tales."

"Sadly, the life of a fisher is quite dull. Your story intrigues me," Simon said, holding out his tankard to be refilled.

After topping it off, Clement crossed his legs and took a sip of his own. "As you wish. I will start. Back when Edward of York first ascended the throne, the French took over Mont Orgueil and ruled Jersey."

Simon nodded. "Yes, I heard."

"Not long after, one of our isle folk set his sights on my home, Meleches Manor, one of the most powerful on the isle. My uncle, a priest, owned it, and I was set to inherit. The captain of the French garrison accused my uncle of treason, confiscated his manor, and gave it to another. Following the siege that ousted the French, that same man fled into exile, leaving my beloved home abandoned and falling into disrepair. Despite my pleas, Governor Harleston refused to restore it to my family. As a result, I was forced to live in poverty. I have since improved myself enough to own this humble manor, and even gained a small voice in the workings of the isle."

"Such an extraordinary tale." Simon held out his tankard and waited for Clement to refill it.

"It is not a tale. It is the truth," Clement said, emptying the first flask and pulling a second one from the basket. "And now, Simon, who are you really?"

The muffled patter on the thatched roof quickened, and the man looked up. "I have already told you, I am Simon, a fisher."

Thunder rumbled, shaking the stable. The animals snorted and pawed at the ground, their bodies slamming against the side of the stall. Simon jumped up to settle them, the blanket slipping from his shoulders. Although the man was about Clement's height, the tunic hung loosely on his slender frame.

When Simon returned, Clement said. "I am helping you, yet you refuse to trust me. I deserve the truth. You claim to be a fisher, but your face and hands betray you. You are no more a fisher than I." Clement's hand clenched the hilt of his dagger. "Your desire for secrecy suggests you are a supporter of Henry Tudor and thus a traitor to the crown. Do you deny it?"

When Simon did not respond, Clement said, "Perhaps I should fetch the constable."

"I beg you, please do not do that."

"So you admit the truth of it?"

Simon nodded his head. "But only in part."

"Tell me." Clement smirked. "Which part am I wrong about?"

"I am no Henry Tudor supporter." Simon paused and gripped his tankard tightly with both hands. "I am Henry Tudor."

Clement stared at Simon. A laugh escaped him—surely this was a jape—but it quickly died as the weight of such a claim settled in. "You must think me daft to fall for such a story. Anyone found supporting or giving aid to Henry Tudor faces serious consequences." Clement shook his head in disbelief. "Your tale is surely a falsehood. Besides, why would Henry Tudor be floundering about in the stormy sea off the coast of Jersey?"

Fear flickered in Simon's eyes. "Perhaps you have not heard about the uprising? My supporters in exile and I attempted to land in England only days ago, but were forced to turn back on account of the storm. Unfortunately, on the journey back to Brittany, I was swept overboard. That is how I have come to be here, a dangerous fugitive in the eyes of King Richard and his allies."

"Why should I not hand you over to the constable?"

"Because I can offer you something better if you help me get back to Brittany," Simon replied. "Something greater than coin, which will be spent in a season."

"And what might that be?"

"What if I could promise you the return of Meleches Manor and a powerful position on the isle? Something that would ensure your name is remembered in the annals of history?" He scrutinized Clement's face, as if trying to read his thoughts. "Would that be worth spiriting me away to Brittany?"

Clement sneered. "I am no fool. Only the king and the governor have the power to grant those."

"You speak truth," Simon said. "What matters is whether you will forgo a certainty now for a greater future reward. It is inevitable—one day I will sit on the throne of England."

Clement's eyes widened, his mouth gaped. "Can it be? Is it really possible that Henry Tudor sits before me?"

"It is." Simon—no—Henry Tudor leaned forward, his voice confident. "What will you choose? To keep the vile King Richard on the throne and remain a nameless subject? Or cast your lot with me and rise to greatness?"

"And if you fail?"

"You would be no worse off. However, the tide is shifting. More and more nobles are turning against Richard. Victory is now a near certainty, but only if you help me. All that is required is your patience," Henry said, "and my safe passage to Brittany."

"If my duplicity is discovered, I shall hang."

"Clement, you are more clever than that. You alone know that I am here—know my true identity. The only one who can betray you is yourself."

Out of excuses, Clement contemplated what his help would

require. The only way to get the man, Henry Tudor, to Brittany, would be by rowing a boat himself.

No small feat.

In summer conditions, it would take ten hours to row to Brittany. But given the vehemence of the storm, the time and the danger would be multiplied. Nor was he an experienced rower, and he doubted Henry was either. What did they know about tides, contrary winds, adverse weather, or navigation? Well, Henry might know a bit more, but Clement would be on his own on the way back. While Henry could promise Clement power and the return of his home, would he survive the journey?

Yet the lure of wealth and power was a strong inducement. He just needed to acquire a boat.

"I must get you away from here lest the servants discover you. I have an empty cottage in St. Martin's parish. Be fore-warned, many people travel the road between here and there. We must devise a plan so we do not find ourselves in the dungeon of Mont Orgueil."

"How far to this cottage?" Henry asked.

"About an hour's walk. If we take the beasts, three quarters of an hour."

"Either way, I will need a disguise. If one person recognizes me, all shall be lost."

Clement shook his head. "I cannot risk going back to the house and looking for more clothes. I fear we must make do with the blankets."

"Should we be detained, we must have a story to keep the curious at bay." Henry stared up at the open rafters and drummed his fingers on his chin. "I heard recent rumors of an outbreak of the Black Death. That would keep any passersby away."

Clement shivered, as anyone would at the mention of the

plague. A vision of his mother arose, the only one who had ever truly loved him, running, laughing, and playing games with him. Days later, her skin darkened, and she drew her last labored breath. He had cried for a week while his father taunted him for being a baby. He was seven then, just a child. How many times had his father, the old bastard, blamed him for her death? Clement jumped up and paced the stable.

He spoke, his tone thoughtful. "That could work. The isle folk know I survived the plague as a child, and no one would dare poke about the cottage."

Henry yawned. "I propose we get some sleep. If we leave at sunrise, I suspect we will encounter fewer people along the road."

While Henry settled down to sleep, Clement rustled up a pitchfork and jammed it between the door and the wall. "This should keep any passersby from seeking shelter here."

When morning broke, the patter of rain on the roof had stopped. Clement removed the pitchfork; the door creaked as he slid it open. To his delight, sunlight filled the stable. God had surely bestowed his blessing on the plans he and Henry had made last night. He nudged Henry awake. "Let us make haste before the place is teeming with peasants and servants."

Henry yawned and stretched, then crumpled in on himself. "I fear I am of little use this morning. My muscles are stiff and sore."

"That will only make our tale more believable," Clement said, as he fetched the saddles and bridles.

The horse stood patiently as Clement tightened the saddle and buckled the bridle. Not so the ass, who kicked and brayed his protest. Clement fetched a crust of bread and fed it to the stubborn beast, whispering and stroking its nose, until it calmed.

When both animals were ready, Clement helped Henry onto the ass. "Lie low over its neck, and I will cover you with the blanket. Stir not, lest the beast unseat you."

Henry made no protest. Taking the reins of the ass, Clement mounted the horse and nudged it forward. The ass plodded obediently behind. They turned northward onto the muddy road leading to St. Martin's parish. Several folks called out greetings and commented on the improved weather, but most looked the other way. Not uncommon in Clement's experience. Since his uncle's untimely death, many shunned him as if he were leprous. But today, he did not care, for he held a secret to which none were privy. When Henry Tudor claimed the throne, and he regained his rightful place, they all would pay. He would see to it.

Mont Orgueil lay ahead. The ass balked as a group of boisterous soldiers passed by, probably on their way to the market in St. Helier. Clement held his breath, hoping they would not ask questions. His newly gained position as a jurat on the Royal Court would give him some standing to resist interrogation, but if something appeared suspicious—

He breathed a sigh of relief when the soldiers passed by acting as if Clement were invisible. Any other day, he would have demanded they pay him deference, but today he welcomed the oversight.

But not five minutes on, Thomas Lempriere, another new fellow jurat, greeted him. "Hoy, Clement! Where are you going with that load? Do you need some assistance?"

Thomas had always been too friendly for Clement's taste, and the sight of Thomas reminded Clement he was due at the

Royal Court in a few days. Fie! It would be impossible to be there if he were making the voyage to Brittany.

"Hoy, Thomas!" Clement said. "Not at all. I am just taking some things to my cottage." He pulled back the reins, bringing the horse to a halt. The ass stopped short, and Clement's eyes widened when a foot slid out from beneath the blanket. His pulse quickened and his stomach clenched. He quickly stilled his visage, hoping Thomas had not noticed.

Thomas's brow furrowed and he stepped forward, hand out, ready to grab the blanket. "Who is that?

Clement waved his hand. "Do not touch. A maidservant of mine has taken ill with the Black Death. I plan to isolate her at the cottage and hope the plague spreads no further."

"Dressed like a man?"

Merde! *I must take more care to guard my tongue.* "For modesty's sake."

Thomas took several steps back. "Anything I can do to help?"

Yes. Clement needed time—and a cockboat.

"Warn anyone who asks to stay clear of the cottage," Clement replied. "Also, if you could make a request to Philippe. Tell him urgent business has arisen and could he delay the verdict hearing by a fortnight." He lowered his voice. "And if you could find someone to lend me their cockboat. My maidservant is nigh death. I shall bury her at sea. It is the best course of action to stop the spread before it begins."

Thomas nodded. "Your prodigious care for our citizenry is admirable. To put your own life at risk goes beyond the call of duty."

Clement touched the brim of his hat. "Pray, do not spread these bad tidings. Perchance this will remain an isolated incident. No need to frighten the populace unnecessarily."

"I am honored to be of help. Once I procure a cockboat, where shall I deliver it?"

Not having thought through that part of the plan, Clement replied, "You are more familiar with St. Martin's Parish's coastline than I. Where do you suggest?"

Thomas squared his shoulders. "The rocky point some distance north of Mont Orgueil. I can anchor the boat on the northward side where it will be out of sight of the random passerby. When all is ready, I will ride by and call out for my dog, Hanish."

"Excellent. Your assistance is invaluable. Such a pity we must keep this to ourselves."

"Knowing I helped save lives is enough for me."

Henry squirmed beneath the blanket. Clement inclined his head. "I do not mean to be rude, but I must move along. My maidservant appears agitated."

"Of course." Thomas's face looked stricken as he made a slight bow.

Clement nudged the horse and, fortunately, the ass did not resist, but followed obediently behind. The corner of Clement's mouth ticked. How easily had Thomas accepted the deception, becoming an unsuspecting participant to a plan that if discovered, could end with all their heads on pikes above the gate of Mont Orgueil.

"Hoy, Clement!" Thomas yelled after him.

Thomas's voice grated on Clement's nerves as he brought the horse to a halt. The ass bumped into the horse's legs, causing it to sidestep. He gasped as the blanket slipped. Henry's hand appeared and grabbed it before it slid away from his body. "Yes, Thomas."

"Perchance you have already heard," Thomas said, with a look of self-importance, "there is word from England that Henry Tudor attempted an invasion. Fortunately, he failed, but should you see him, he is to be handed over to the governor forthwith."

"Gramercy for your tidings. I had not heard. But then, it is highly unlikely that Henry Tudor would come to Jersey."

"I am sure you are right," Thomas replied. "Carry on."

When Clement and Henry reached the cottage, Clement scanned the landscape. Satisfied they were alone, he pulled the blanket off Henry and helped him off the ass, hustling him inside.

The cottage was comprised of two rooms; a public room containing a square table surrounded by four chairs in the center, a dilapidated sideboard under the window, and a few bits of kindling stacked on the ash-covered hearth. A separate chamber contained a bed, a washstand, and a wardrobe.

Henry looked about, clearly unaccustomed to living in such humble surroundings, but at least the cottage was off the beaten path, a safe place to wait until they could set off for Brittany.

Clement pointed to the chamber. "That will provide a hiding place should anyone come by." He crossed to the sideboard and rummaged inside. "I thought my uncle kept a container of red paint. A cross on the door will keep folks from prying into our business."

"Or announce someone is here," Henry replied, looking none too pleased at the idea.

"The presence of my horse and the ass have already done so."

"Checking on your own property will not raise suspicion, but the sight of a red cross announcing the Black Death would only scare folks. Before long, the entire isle would be abuzz with gossip. Best to let well enough alone."

Clement nodded. "Take the bed, Your Grace. Surely, you are still tired from your ordeal? We must be prepared to leave at a moment's notice."

Henry inclined his head and excused himself, entering the chamber and closing the door behind him.

Clement sat at the table and surveyed the cottage. Other than the accumulation of cobwebs and dust, the cottage had changed little from when he had lived here—that is, after Meleches Manor had been confiscated and before Wilhelmina had tricked him into marriage. So often his life had been subject to the whims of others. But this time, he was in control, and it felt good.

He shivered with excitement. *Henry Tudor's life—nay, the future of England rests in my hands.* If they survived this journey, and Henry succeeded in taking the throne, he would regain, nay, earn, his rightful place in history. To walk again through the doors of Meleches Manor, to have the acclaim of his peers, and the undying gratitude of the king—it was difficult to take it all in.

Hopefully, it would not be long before Henry ascended the throne. Until then, he would be bursting to share his secret, yet he must continue on as if nothing had changed.

That is unless Henry played him false. His hand wrapped around the hilt of his dagger. The secrecy of all this meant that Henry could later deny Clement's claim, pretend none of it had happened. That he, Clement Le Hardy, had fabricated a story for his own gain.

Unable to remain seated, Clement sprang up from the chair and paced the room, stopping often to peer out the window. What was taking Thomas so long? He sat again, his nerves frayed, willing himself to be patient. It would take Thomas time to acquire a cockboat.

As the sun set, the sky streaked with pinks, purples and oranges, and a cry of "Hanish" sounded in the distance. Some of the tension left Clement's body knowing the plan was coming together. They would wait for the cover of darkness to venture from the cottage, hopefully avoiding detection.

The chamber door creaked, and Henry appeared. "I heard the signal. I am ready."

"Another hour and it will be dark. We will make our way to the point on foot. The animals will draw too much attention."

The two waited in silence. Clement suspected Henry was just as nervous as he was about the upcoming voyage. The weather might be calm now, but there was no guarantee it would hold. Or that they would make it to deep waters without being discovered. Not that taking a boat out at night was illegal, but it would surely draw attention and maybe investigation.

When darkness fell, the two men slipped out of the cottage into the night, with nary a lantern or torch, using only the stars and a sliver of moon to light the way. They stumbled along the unfamiliar paths, stopping often to ensure they were headed eastward. Finally, they reached the point, finding the cockboat discreetly hidden just as Thomas had promised.

Together, Clement and Henry pushed it into the water. The scrape of the sand on the hull was replaced by gasps as the cold water wrapped around their legs. Once settled in the boat, they rowed far out into the Channel, careful the oars made no sound as they dipped into and pulled out of the water.

Turning south, they glided past Mont Orgueil, alight with torches. In the bailey, the soldiers who manned their posts along the battlements looked like shadows. A cloud slipped over the moon. Clement sucked in his breath, expecting a shout of discovery. None came.

Once past the castle, the cloud drifted on, and moonlight illuminated the water. There was no turning back. The die had been cast, and, for good or ill, Clement had thrown in his lot with Henry Tudor.

Author's Note

If Clement had made a different choice—if he had handed the fugitive Henry Tudor over to the governor—Henry would likely have been shipped back to England and executed for treason. Imagine if there had been no Tudor dynasty. The world would have been deprived of Henry VIII.

One inconsequential man. One choice. And consequences that echo even today.

This fictionalized encounter between Henry Tudor and Clement Le Hardy is considered controversial history; some claim it is untrue. However, it is recounted in the annals of Jersey history and memorialized on the tomb of one of Clement Le Hardy's descendants, Sir Thomas Le Hardy, interned in Westminster Abbey, London, in 1732.

The story of the French Occupation and how Clement's uncle was stripped of his estate can be found in C.V. Lee's novel, *Token of Betrayal*.

Did Henry Tudor keep his promises to Clement? Find out in the novel *Betrayal of Trust* by C.V. Lee.

EIGHT
BY LINDA ULLESEIT

Harriet Scott and the other laundresses, free Black and enslaved, knelt on the bank of the Mississippi River with their buckets. Harriet pushed aside ice chunks to scoop up the muddy water. She tucked her frozen hand under her armpit, trying to warm it before carrying the bucket up the riverbank. Her seven-year-old daughter, Eliza, stretched out her arms and spun in a circle nearby. Eliza loved being outside, but it was time to get to work. Harriet checked on her toddler, Lizzie, thankfully asleep in a nest of blankets, and waved to Eliza. Her older daughter helped with the buckets and tended the fire under the big oaken tub.

Leaving the frigid river water to settle its dirt to the bottom of the bucket, Harriet peered into the wheelbarrow full of white clothes that had been soaking since Saturday. She'd used lemon on the stains and was pleased to see that it appeared to be working.

When the silt had settled from the water, Harriet carefully

scooped the clean water into the second big tub over the fire. She made two more trips to the river to fill buckets before she had enough clean water.

Nearby, her friend Milly tended her own fire. She caught Harriet's eye and nodded toward Lucy, an enslaved girl whose mother they both remembered. Harriet thought her about thirteen or so. The girl looked unsure as she filled her buckets with water.

"Lucy's papa was sold downriver when their master died," Milly said. "When the mistress died, she was supposed to free Lucy, like she promised, but that didn't happen. So her mama ran away to Illinois." Milly waved at the far side of the Mississippi River.

"I heard Lucy's mama sued for her freedom, won, and moved to Illinois for good last year."

"It wasn't that easy," Milly said. She nodded at Lucy. "Lucy was given to one of the mistress's daughters, and now she's doing laundry. She's never done that before."

Staring into her boiling water, Harriet thought about Lucy's mother running away and leaving her daughter behind. Harriet could never do that. But she couldn't imagine her daughters being sold or rented away from her, either. She took the white clothes out of the rinse water and put them in the hot water, adding lye soap.

Milly nodded to Eliza. "You can't protect her after she turns eight."

In a matter of months, Eliza would turn eight years old, the age when Mrs. Emerson could sell or rent her to someone else.

"You don't need to tell me that." In an effort to keep fear out of her voice, Harriet's tone sounded sharp. Milly was a dear friend, but she couldn't keep her opinions to herself. Secretly, Harriet thought Milly's confidence stemmed from her status as a free Black.

Not that Harriet and her husband hadn't talked about escaping. After all, she and Dred had mostly been left on their own both at Fort Snelling and in St. Louis. No master had beaten them or ordered them around. Still, when Dr. Emerson had called them south to St. Louis from the fort in free territory, they had to come.

When Dred was hired out to Captain Bainbridge of the U.S. Army and taken to Louisiana, they clung to each other the night before he left, making desperate plans to flee that became practical plans to reunite after the war. There was no guarantee Captain Bainbridge would ever bring Dred back to St. Louis, but Harriet couldn't consider running away and leaving no word of where she was. It could be worse—unless, of course, Dred didn't come back. Or Eliza was sold.

Milly exclaimed, "Oh dear sweet Lord!" She leaped to Lucy's aid just a moment before Harriet.

They were too late. Lucy had poured two buckets of river water into her tub, which was already boiling. Harriet cringed to see the mud mixing with the water and white clothes.

"The water's too dirty if you don't let it settle, hon," Milly said.

Lucy's eyes widened.

"Let's see how bad it is," Harriet said. She used Lucy's wooden paddle to lift one chemise out of the muddy water. The warm bundle steamed in the cold air.

"It's dirtier than when I brought it," Lucy wailed.

"We'll help you rewash them," Harriet said.

Leaving Eliza to stir their laundry, Harriet lifted the clothes out of Lucy's tub one garment at a time, putting them into the empty rinse tub. Milly rummaged through her box of laundry supplies. "I have liquid paraffin and a bit of stale bread. They are best on oil and grease stains, Lucy, but they might work on mud. You have alcohol, Harriet?"

"Yes, and lemon juice. I'll get them." Harriet retrieved the items from her own box as Lucy wrung her hands.

"I'm gonna show you how to do this," Milly said, "but I'm not going to do it for you."

Lucy nodded.

Harriet picked up a chemise and began rubbing it with lemon juice. Milly started Lucy with the stale bread, blotting the chemise so the bread would pull the muddy brown out of the fabric. She picked up the paraffin herself, applied it to the spot, let it dry, then rubbed it off. The three worked in silence for the better part of an hour with limited success.

Finally, Harriet stood. "I need to get back to mine." She made sure baby Lizzie was asleep, then joined Eliza, who had filled their second tub with clean water. They transferred the heavy, wet clothes from the hot water to the cold water tub to rinse. The air felt even colder against Harriet's exertion-warmed skin, and when she drew a deep breath, she could feel it icing her throat. Eliza didn't have a warm coat and wore only a light sweater. Harriet was glad the girl liked to dance. It kept her warm.

"There's nothing more to do, child," Milly said. "River mud is relentless. I'm sorry."

Lucy started to cry. "I have to bring dirty laundry back?"

Milly patted her shoulder in comfort, but had to get back to her own tub, which was beginning to boil over. Harriet helped Lucy rinse and wring out the dirty clothes and lay them back in the tub. They emptied Lucy's wash tub and rinsed the mud out of it. Lucy gathered her dirty laundry and trudged back to her mistress's house.

Smaller than Harriet and a few years older, Milly's wiry arms had lost none of their strength. She turned her pile of clothes inside out and put them in her tub of hot wash water, scrubbing some of them on a washboard.

Milly said, "You ever have any thoughts of suing for freedom?"

"I lived in free territory for five years," Harriet reminded her friend. "My owner freed me." But not Dred. And neither of them had any proof of their status. Harriet put her wooden dolly stick into the tub and stirred, mixing soap into the clothing. But suing for freedom was not something one did on impulse. Such a lawsuit invited the master's retaliation and had many unknown dangers, including jail.

Milly scrubbed a man's shirt on a washboard, panting with the exertion. "But Mrs. Russell believes she owns both of you?"

"No," Harriet said. "When Dr. Emerson died, Mrs. Emerson became Dred's owner. She hired us out to Mrs. Russell." Their lives were basically unsupervised, which was almost like being free, but their wages went to Colonel Sanford, Mrs. Emerson's father. Mrs. Russell provided them a place to live and one set of clothes a year. Harriet took in extra laundry to make money they could keep.

Milly busied herself with the second wash on her pile of laundry. Harriet wrapped a solid chunk of indigo into a cloth ball and dipped it into the rinse water with her white clothes. The resulting blue color would balance the yellow left by the soap and result in whiter garments.

On the following Monday at the river, Lucy was nowhere to be seen.

"I heard her mistress talked about selling her, so Lucy ran," Milly said.

Everyone at the river knew someone who had been sold and felt the pain of forced separation from a loved one. Harriet looked at Eliza and imagined the terrible rending of her heart if Mrs. Emerson sold her. She picked up Lizzie and held her tight, knowing Eliza would squirm at such a show of affection in public.

"She'll run to her Mama?" Harriet asked.

"She got nowhere else to go," Milly said. "If she lives in Illinois for ninety days, she can sue for her freedom under Illinois law."

"Ninety days is a long time to hide," Harriet said.

The network of laundresses learned that Lucy's mother had filed a lawsuit for her daughter's freedom. Harriet and Milly were thrilled. That is, until Lucy was returned to St. Louis and jailed. When Lucy's case finally came to trial, she was freed after one day of testimony and deliberation.

"Her mama came and took her home to Illinois," Milly reported.

"Good for them." Harriet skimmed the clean water out of her bucket into the wash tub.

Lizzie, now two years old, sat inside an empty laundry basket playing with a wooden ring that had been Eliza's. Lizzie was a constant reminder of how long Dred had been gone. There was no word how the war was going, or if Captain Bainbridge was even still with the army in Texas.

"Your husband will be surprised how much this one has grown," Milly said, nodding at Lizzie.

"You're reading my mind," Harriet said with a sigh. "And Eliza has become quite the helper." She missed laughing with Dred about the girls, sharing meals, and talking about her day, even if it didn't vary much.

Eliza smiled. "I can play with Lizzie *and* help with the laundry and cooking." Her pride echoed Harriet's.

On a Thursday in March, Harriet was ironing. She had one iron on a clean frying pan warming on a fire grate while she used one that had already been heated. Exertion and the temperature in the stifling room led Harriet to opening the door, letting in cooler air. She set the hot iron down to stretch her back for a moment, leaning backwards and staring out the open doorway. Her breath caught as a man, silhouetted against the spring sun, appeared in the doorway.

"You're a sight for sore eyes," he said.

Her heart sang as she ran to embrace the man she loved that she hadn't seen in almost two years. "Oh, Dred, I'm happy to see you," she said, the words muffled against his dusty coat. "Is the war over?" Harriet frowned. Surely she'd have heard?

Dred's lips tightened. "No. Captain Bainbridge sent me back. He needs someone younger."

Harriet could see the angry hurt in his eyes, but she could also see gray in his close-cropped black hair. Dred was fifty-one. Harriet knew that she had begun to feel more tired at the end of the day than she used to, and she counted her years as twenty-eight. She squeezed his hands. "I'm glad you're back."

Harriet turned to pick up Lizzie, who stirred from sleep and rubbed her eyes. Dred's jaw dropped. Lizzie had been an infant when he left. She'd become a little girl. Harriet smiled, but Lizzie clung to her mother.

"She's beautiful like her mama," Dred said.

"Mrs. Russell wanted Eliza to help in the kitchen this morning. She'll be back soon."

Dred's eyes searched Harriet's. "She'll be eight in October."

"I know." The thought of that upcoming birthday dampened her spirits. Harriet put Lizzie down and gave her a doll she'd made from rags. She resumed ironing.

"I'll go get cleaned up," Dred said. "Maybe I should've done that first, but I couldn't wait to see you." He kissed Harriet lightly and left, heading for their rooms behind the Russell house.

That night, the family ate together. Harriet hummed as she served dinner, well pleased that her husband and daughters were all at the same table once again. Eliza chattered away about how she'd helped with making the pork, cowpeas, and cornbread. Harriet poured molasses over the cornbread as a special treat welcoming Dred home. She wished the four of them could stay just like this forever.

The next morning, Harriet and Eliza folded the mended, washed, and ironed laundry for the week. Eliza took the Russell's laundry into the house while Harriet delivered laundry to her other customers. She smiled as she walked, enjoying the gentle spring day and the promise of a complete family at home that night.

Returning to the Russell's, though, she passed the courthouse. It was only a few blocks from where she lived and worked, and she sometimes heard the commotion when they held slave auctions on the courthouse steps. Today, however, she could imagine what would happen if her husband and daughter were up there. Dred would be classified as "elderly" and would fetch no better a price than his young daughter. Heart in her throat, Harriet hurried past, the echo of the auctioneer's call following and mocking her.

That evening, after the girls were in bed, Dred took her hand. "I've got some money put aside from my army pay. I want to purchase my freedom from Mrs. Russell."

Harriet nodded as her heart leaped. "Mr. Taliaferro freed me. Purchase your freedom, and we can ensure the girls stay with us."

Dred shook his head. "You know Mrs. Emerson believes you

48

and the girls are hers." Harriet's lips tightened. Dred continued, "Let me go alone to Mrs. Russell. It might help to make her believe that you're already free."

Harriet paced the dirt yard while Eliza and Lizzie played. She couldn't concentrate on laundry with her whole mind wrapped around Dred's conversation with Mrs. Russell.

Not even an hour had passed before he returned. Harriet's stomach flipped when she saw his face. He certainly didn't show joy at emancipation.

Dred took her hand and led her inside. "She refused. I told her I knew an army officer who would vouch for me, that would tell her I have the money. She told me I was practically free anyway, and that was good enough." He stopped to take a shaky breath. "She said under Missouri law an elderly slave can't just be freed. She would be responsible for my continued support even if she freed me." His shoulders slumped.

"Oh, Dred." Harriet filled with disappointed anger. She could see defeat in her husband's eyes. He didn't want to be seen as elderly, and he wanted to legally free them all. Maybe Mrs. Emerson couldn't make the decision herself. A white woman in Missouri couldn't free a slave without two white men to give oaths. That meant her husband and her father. And Colonel Sanford, Mrs. Emerson's father, never met a slave he didn't enjoy abusing.

Harriet continued to mull over their situation as she collected the next week's laundry. Sitting on the front step of her home, taking advantage of the light, Harriet examined every garment and sheet for tears and mended them. The blare of brass instruments drew her attention to the Russell home nearby. It was a military band, no doubt just returned from the campaign in Mexico. Harriet saw Mrs. Russell's daughter, Almira, at an upstairs window. At sixteen, Almira was charming and popular. Harriet saw the young woman laugh at the men in the band and flirtatiously toss one of her gloves out the window. An officer caught it and bowed toward Almira, who laughed again.

Lucy had been given to her new mistress when the young woman wed. Harriet wondered if Mrs. Russell had any such plans for Eliza. It wasn't unusual to pass on children of slaves like that, but Harriet wasn't a slave. It did no good to protest that she and her children were free, though, if they had no way to prove it. Would Mrs. Russell try to give Eliza to Almira?

Finally, a week after Dred's return, she confronted him. "Let's sue, Dred." The idea had been lurking in the shadows of her mind since Lucy won her freedom. "If we sue now, we might have freedom before Eliza's birthday."

He looked at her, despair in his eyes. "Our family is more secure now."

Harriet knew he was afraid to think about it. "I know free Black laundresses that work as hard as I do at the river," she said, "and it's true their lives aren't any easier just for being free. You know what, though? They're secure in the knowledge that their families are intact and will stay that way. That's what I want for us, Dred."

"I do, too," he assured her.

"We can't let Eliza be sold." A chill ran down Harriet's spine.

"If we file suit, we won't be welcome at the Russell's. The Emersons couldn't hire us out to anyone else, either. We might be put in jail until the trial." Dred paused, his brow furrowed. "I know," Harriet said. He didn't know how many times she'd considered the options herself. She'd ask Milly to watch out for Eliza and Lizzie should she and Dred be jailed.

"Let's think about it," Dred said. Did she hear a hint of optimism in his voice?

"Maybe we can talk to Lucy's lawyer and see if he thinks we've got a case," Harriet said.

Two weeks later, the white lawyer, Mr. Murdoch, led Harriet and Dred Scott into his sparsely furnished office. They settled themselves near his desk. Harriet's chair rocked on uneven legs.

"Tell me about your situation," Mr. Murdoch said. He wrote *April 1846* on the legal pad before him.

Dred looked to Harriet. She said, "My master was Mr. Taliaferro, the Indian Agent at Fort Snelling in Minnesota. He brought me there, into free territory, where I lived for five years. He always said he'd free me."

"Your marriage proves that," Mr. Murdoch said, jotting a note on his pad. "Even in Wisconsin Territory slaves can't legally marry."

"Mr. Taliaferro freed me so I could marry Dred. He even performed the ceremony. Dred belonged to Dr. Emerson, though, so I worked for the doctor. When the doctor passed away unexpectedly, he left a hastily written will that didn't mention either of us at all. But he knew I was free and wished to free Dred."

The lawyer turned to Dred. "You were at Fort Snelling, too. Are you claiming residence in a free territory?" When Dred affirmed this, he continued. "But neither of you have paperwork? The truth is that without paperwork you are enslaved." He leaned forward. "You wish to file a lawsuit?"

Dred looked at Harriet. "Yes. How do we go about it?"

"I can take care of it. Two lawsuits, actually, one for each of you. We'll need witnesses to establish your residence at the fort. You also need to decide which master you will sue. Which one has limited your freedom the most?"

Dred lifted an eyebrow at Harriet, who shrugged. According to law, Mrs. Emerson owned them. Colonel Sanford, her father, collected their wages and advised his daughter. Mrs. Russell had hired them and was responsible for their day-to-day duties. Any one of them was a possibility. "Mrs. Emerson." Dred spoke in a firm tone.

"Filing suit is considered an act of resistance. Are you prepared to do jail time if they decide to arrest you?"

Swallowing hard, Harriet nodded.

"Mrs. Emerson, to my knowledge, has no plans to sell you south. And you've never tried to run. That might keep you out of jail." Mr. Murdoch put the papers in front of them, and they placed their marks on them.

The Scotts left the lawyer's office weak with terrified euphoria. There was no going back now.

They had to leave Mrs. Russell's property if they claimed their freedom, so they hurried to collect their meager belongings and their daughters, not wanting to encounter the Russells when they heard about the lawsuit. Eliza put up no objections when told to gather her things. "I've got Lizzie," she said. Her voice was mature beyond her years, which made Harriet both proud and scared.

They had no money for a boarding house but found a temporary place with Reverend Meacham at the African Church. Harriet continued as a laundress and easily picked up more customers. Dred ran errands for people arriving at the busy St. Louis dock.

Mrs. Emerson hired a lawyer who moved to dismiss the lawsuit. Then nothing. Mr. Murdoch warned the Scotts that the court proceedings would take time. As the days passed, Harriet stopped looking for news about their case. She couldn't stay in a state of anticipation forever. No word came from Mrs. Emerson, who claimed to be their owner, or from Mrs. Russell, who had rented them. It was as if the Scotts had gone and left no ripple in their households.

Eliza's birthday in October fell on a perfect fall day. Harriet woke her daughter with a kiss as usual. Harriet could hardly contain her delight at the surprise she had for the child. She'd managed to get an unblemished apple and polished it with a cloth until it looked like a wax model. "Happy birthday, sweetheart," she said.

Eliza responded with a sleepy smile.

"I have a special treat just for you," Harriet said. She pulled out the apple and handed it to Eliza, whose eyes widened. She'd never had an entire apple to herself. Harriet held her tight. The day was a milestone, one that stiffened Harriet's resolve to continue fighting to prove her legal freedom and keep her daughters free. Dred's lawsuit would free him, and they could be a family.

Eliza put the apple in her skirt pocket. "I'm going to enjoy just having it," she said, "and I'll eat it at a special time."

All day, Harriet felt burdened by the importance of the day. An eighth birthday was such a minor thing for white children. She didn't remember her own eighth birthday, but she'd been sold to Mr. Taliaferro shortly afterwards. For the first time, Harriet wondered if her mother had felt similar reservations about Harriet's eighth birthday. Her stomach twisted. Eliza's eighth birthday was the most terrifying milestone Harriet had ever encountered. She had to be strong, but first she had to endure the day.

At the river, Milly took one look at Harriet and narrowed her eyes. "You look like a ghost be sittin' on your grave." Eliza's happy humming caught her ear. "Daughter's in a good mood." She peered at Harriet. "Oh. It's October. Could the child be eight today?"

Harriet moaned. "Don't say it out loud, Milly."

"Won't make it less true," Milly said. "Most slaves aren't allowed to celebrate birthdays, and many don't even know when their birthday is. When I was freed, I chose that day to be my birthday." She shrugged.

It was true. Harriet wasn't sure of her birthday either. But Eliza *was* free, born in the free Iowa territory to a freed black woman. Harriet knew that to be true in her heart even if no one else but Dred agreed.

When Eliza carried two buckets of water from the river by herself, Harriet glowed with pride. How strong her girl was! But any show of strength would increase her value and her likelihood to be sold. She snapped at Eliza, causing the girl's eyes to widen, and instantly felt remorse.

Watching her finally eat the apple she cherished, Harriet realized how much of the washday chores Eliza had come to manage. In addition to tending the fire and her little sister, Eliza carried water and worked on stubborn stains that hadn't come out in the rinse. She fetched heavier wood pieces for Milly's fire, too, making her indispensable and causing Harriet's heart to constrict.

The benefit of each excruciating moment was that anxiety over Eliza's birthday overshadowed the lack of progress on their case. Butterflies swarmed in her stomach all day. They stilled only when Dred came home from a day of running errands with no money but two loaves of fresh bread. She cut thick slices and toasted them, spreading a bit of butter on top for a treat. When the birthday girl and her sister were asleep, Dred and Harriet sat in their front room, silent, holding hands. Nothing needed to be said. They had discussed their anxieties over and over. Waiting with each other comforted them both.

In November, Mrs. Emerson entered a plea of not guilty to the charge of assault on the Scotts' liberty. The case would go to trial. It felt like a very tiny step of progress. With only one judge, the courthouse was busy, and the Scotts could do nothing but wait and hope.

Days were busy with laundry, but Harriet's evenings left too much time to worry. One evening, she picked up a basket of the family's mending. "Come by the fire, Eliza," she said. "You know how to hem. Now you'll learn to fix a seam."

Eliza smiled. She loved helping and learning new things; truly a daughter to be proud of. Harriet threaded a needle and turned a skirt inside out.

"See where the seam has pulled open? Start to one side of the rip and take tiny stitches."

Eliza sighed. "Always tiny stitches."

"Take the time to do it right and you won't have to do it again," her mother admonished.

Later that month, Judge Krum ruled against a free Black man who'd been arrested for living in Missouri without a license. As free Blacks swarmed to acquire licenses, Harriet felt true freedom slipping away. If she and Dred won their case, but were unable to get a license, their freedom would still be in danger. And so would Eliza's and Lizzie's.

Harriet made a new rag doll for Eliza's Christmas gift, and gave the old doll to Lizzie, who was into everything and needed distraction. She admired Eliza's gentleness with her sister and the way she cared for her new toy.

On New Year's Day 1847, the courthouse steps held the annual spectacle of slave-leasing. Harriet couldn't block the harsh call of the auctioneer or the mental image of Eliza or Dred being on those steps.

Her spirits fell further into despair when Judge Krum resigned, leaving the circuit court with no judge for two months. Then their lawyer, Mr. Murdoch, left Missouri for good just before a spring snowstorm blanketed the city. Eliza played outside, throwing snowballs at Lizzie, who tried to run but kept falling into the snowbank.

"Dred, what will we do?" Harriet asked. Through the

window, she saw Lizzie dodge a snowball and taunt her sister. Both of them laughed with delight. She never wanted to see those smiles fade. "We simply can't give up."

"It seems the only choice is for me to go see Mr. Blow," Dred said.

Mr. Blow had been Dred's original owner, the one who sold him to Mr. Emerson, and he was very supportive of Dred's bid for freedom. A family member took on the case, and another pledged to pay for court costs. The 1847 court session opened in May and depositions were scheduled. But it was June before Dred's case came to trial, eighteen months after they filed the lawsuit. Yet, there was no word about Harriet's separate lawsuit, the one that would guarantee the children's freedom.

Harriet left Eliza at home with Lizzie on the days of the trial. "You are in charge," she said. "Keep the door locked and don't go out."

Eliza nodded her head. "I'm very responsible, Mama."

Harriet hugged her close. "Oh, I know, sweetheart."

The Scotts walked to the courthouse, which was under construction. During the trial, workers built walls, porticos, and columns around them as the Scotts watched the trial from the second-story balcony. Harriet's heart was full of hope, but she clutched Dred's arm in apprehension as her mind ran over all the terrible possibilities.

Their new lawyer had no problem proving the couple's residence in a free territory, but he also needed to prove that someone had confined them against their will. Mr. Russell took the stand on the second day of the trial. Harriet's jaw dropped as she listened to his testimony.

"I never hired Dred Scott from Mrs. Emerson," Mr. Russell said.

"That's a lie," Dred muttered.

"How can he lie under oath?" Harriet asked, twisting her hands in her lap.

Their case claimed that Mrs. Emerson had deprived them of liberty. With no legal connection between Mrs. Emerson and Mr. Russell, though, the case fell apart. The jury ruled against Dred.

Their lawyer moved for a new trial and the judge granted it.

Harriet and Dred hurried home to their daughters in silence. It wasn't until that evening that they were able to talk about the trial.

"We lost," Dred said.

"We have to go through this again," Harriet said softly. The girls were in bed in a separate room, but the walls were thin. Harriet and Dred sat on a worn couch in the front room that had a kitchen and table at one end.

When the fall term resumed, Dred decided to once again sue Mrs. Emerson. They would need Mrs. Emerson to testify to the relationship between the Russells and Emersons with regard to Dred. But it was a bad time to file a new lawsuit. The St. Louis Circuit Court was being audited, delaying cases even further. At least it gave Judge Hamilton time to look over the docket and realize he'd neglected Harriet's case the previous spring.

One evening at their home, Harriet fed the fire and settled into the sofa with Dred.

"The lawyer says your case was never submitted to the jury," Dred said. "To fix that, he's copied all the details from my case into yours. Congratulations. You've also had a ruling against you."

"So much for my day in court," Harriet said. They both laughed. What else could they do?

"At least the record shows that we both have been granted a new trial," Dred said.

Christmas Day was cold and cloudy. It was the second

Christmas without a box from an owner that would give them new clothes for the upcoming year. They lived on the extra laundry Harriet did, as their labor still earned money for the Emersons.

Harriet showed Eliza how to let out the hem of her dress until there was no hem left. She had no way to make the girl's shoes bigger, though. Lizzie was now three and could no longer wear a baby dress. Dred went to Mrs. Blow to ask for help but returned with nothing.

"She said I asked for too much," he told Harriet in disbelief.

"Milly says even the stray dogs in St. Louis can tell a well-dressed black person from a hired-out shabby slave. They bark more." Harriet tried for a humorous tone but failed.

The year turned to 1848, and on a cold day in February, Milly called to Harriet as soon as she arrived at the river with her laundry tubs, saying, "Did you hear? Colonel Sanford died!"

The colonel, Mrs. Emerson's father and a staunch slave owner, had supported his daughter in opposing Dred and Harriet's cases. While Harriet couldn't mourn his passing, it didn't seem right to celebrate, either. "This might push things along," she told Milly.

Mrs. Emerson appeared personally at the courthouse soon after the funeral for her father. Dred heard about it from an enslaved man he knew at Sanford's farm.

"She sold her land in Iowa for cash," Dred told Harriet. "She also petitioned the court to compel us to be hired out for work."

Harriet stirred the grits on the stove. "How can she do that while we are involved in a lawsuit?"

A sharp knock at their door forestalled Dred's answer. The sheriff entered. Ignoring the children, he said, "I've come to take you both into custody."

"What?" Harriet's answer was automatic. She'd been dreading this for over a year.

The sheriff motioned to Eliza and Lizzie. "They come, too."

Harriet's heart froze. Did this mean they would hire out Eliza, too?

Despite Dred's protests, the sheriff took all four of them to jail. The jailer separated Dred, taking him to the men's section of the jail. Harriet and her daughters were put into an eight foot square cell with a stone floor and a single dirty buffalo robe for all of them. Light trickled through a narrow window in the high wall.

For a year, the family lived on two meals a day and sporadic heat from a stove in the hallway. Eliza entertained Harriet by encouraging Lizzie to dance. When they were tired, Harriet enveloped the girls in her arms and sang "Go to Sleepy," the lullaby her mother had sung to her.

In March of 1849, the jailer released Harriet and the girls, now ten and four. They reunited with Dred outside the jail.

"Our new lawyers signed a bond for us to get us out," Dred told them. "We'll be hired out and we have to find our own living arrangements."

That spring, the Mississippi River flooded, a cholera plague swept the city, and a fire destroyed fifteen blocks from the river to the courthouse. In the middle of June, thunderstorms attacked the city, further impeding the court. Harriet expressed dismay at the tragedies but couldn't help her disappointment at the lack of progress on their case. Cholera had run its course by fall, but the court docket remained full.

Harriet taught Lizzie how to sort laundry, her mind turning back to when she'd taught Eliza.

"Can I show her how to work the stains, Mama?" Eliza asked, fingering a white chemise with a brown spot.

"Yes, of course. Start with lemon." Harriet's pride in her older daughter knew no limits. Was there a more perfect child anywhere?

Finally, Harriet and Dred got a trial in January of 1850. The lawyers went back and forth arguing the same points they'd been arguing for years. Harriet let her mind wander, dreaming of a future that she controlled. Beside her, Dred stared at the judge as if his eyes could control the verdict. Their lawyer had taken a deposition from Mrs. Russell that proved the link with Mrs. Emerson. When the jury adjourned to decide on the verdict, Harriet and Dred locked hands. Without words, they communicated every bit of hope and fear that remained within them.

By the time the jury returned, Harriet and Dred were calm. As the twelve men settled into their seats, though, emotion surged in Harriet—relief that it would be over mixed with apprehension at the result. The foreman stood to read the verdict.

"Oh, Dred," she whispered.

He clasped her hand tightly, the clamminess of his palm revealing that he, too, was anxious.

The foreman stood. Harriet held her breath.

"How say you?" the judge asked.

"We the jury find Mrs. Irene Emerson guilty of impinging on the freedom of Dred and Harriet Scott."

They'd won! Relief and delight suffused Harriet, leaving her legs too wobbly to stand. She could see the same emotions reflected in Dred. Harriet longed to glare at Mrs. Emerson or walk haughtily by Mrs. Russell, but neither of them were in the courtroom. Mrs. Emerson had moved to Massachusetts and remarried. Mrs. Russell was swept up in preparations for the social event of the year—Almira's wedding ten days later.

The Scotts moved into a house near Milly, in a neighborhood of alleyways north of the city where mostly free Blacks lived. Harriet continued working as a laundress, and Dred swept the lawyer's offices. Eliza and Lizzie helped Harriet. For the first time, every penny they earned went to their own family.

It wasn't long before Mrs. Emerson's lawyer filed an appeal on her behalf. The lawyers agreed that Harriet and Dred's individual cases were so closely tied that they would go forward treating it as a single case. Harriet's pride in their victory evaporated. They were not yet legally free.

Now that Eliza was twelve, Harriet taught her how to make the lye soap needed for the laundry. They poured hot water over ashes and drippings, catching it in a large kettle. "Now this needs to be dripped into this trough," Harriet told her daughter. They stood in the kitchen of their small house. Eliza, well acquainted with tending fire, kept the water hot as Harriet added grease and fat to it.

"When is it ready, Mama?" Eliza asked.

"We boil it down, now, until it clumps and sinks to the bottom. Then we cool it and cut it into chunks. By tomorrow it will be dry and ready to use." Harriet arched her aching lower back and rubbed sore muscles in her arms. "You're a big help," she said to Eliza.

At the river the following week, Eliza proudly held out a bar of the soap she'd made to Milly, who exclaimed, "How wonderful! I remember when you were just starting to tend the fire."

Eliza poked her sister. "That's Lizzie's job now."

Lizzie, deep in concentrating on the fire, didn't answer.

"Harriet, you're lucky to have these helpers. None of us are getting younger," Milly said. Sweat ran down the older woman's brow.

"I'm proud of them," Harriet said. "They're free and they're mine." Her words were hollow, though. Mrs. Emerson's appeal loomed over them.

For two years the Scotts lived free until the Missouri Supreme Court revoked their freedom in March of 1852. The court no longer recognized residence in free territory as grounds for freedom in Missouri.

After hearing the news, Dred paced the kitchen, expounding on their situation as Harriet cooked their sparse evening meal. The girls sat at the table, sewing and listening to their parents. Eliza, now thirteen, repaired seams with neat stitches. Lizzie, now seven, fixed hems. Occasionally, she sucked a finger she'd stabbed with her needle.

"We have to sue again," Dred said. "Mrs. Emerson isn't even in Missouri anymore! She's remarried and I have no idea what her name is now. Her father's dead, so her brother, Mr. John Sanford, is supposedly in charge of us, I guess." He ran a hand through dark hair now liberally sprinkled with gray.

"I've never even seen the man," Harriet said. She glanced at her daughters. "It's more complicated now, Dred. Eliza will never pass for a young girl anymore, and Lizzie will be eight soon. Maybe it's time for Milly to take them."

Dred paused to look at his precious daughters. Eliza radiated the calm assurance of a young woman. Lizzie, still as gangly as a colt, kicked her feet a bit as she sewed. Both of them were old enough to understand the complexities of a lawsuit this time around. "Have Milly settle them somewhere they can't be found. Lawyer says we have to sue in federal court this time. It's a bigger deal."

"We must hide what we value most," Harriet said. She kept her eyes down, pretending to focus on the grits in the pot to hide her welling tears. She understood why he wanted the girls to hide, but she'd miss them so much. "Milly will take them deep into the free Black neighborhood at Chouteau's Mill Creek."

Dred resumed pacing. "We'll sue Mr. Sanford as the only representative of his family still in Missouri. I'll talk to the lawyer tomorrow."

By the fall of 1852, the lawyer filed one lawsuit for the entire family in federal court. Dred continued working at a whitewashing job, which did not require speed or strength. That made it a good fit for Dred, who was now sixty. Harriet continued to take in washing. They knew it would take a long time for the case to come to trial. But almost two more years passed for a trial that had no witnesses or testimony. In March of 1854, Judge Robert Wells declared that by law all four Scotts were the property of John Sanford.

Their only recourse was an appeal to the United States Supreme Court. Dred's lawyer found a Washington, D. C. lawyer to take the case, one who'd never met the Scotts. The appeal was filed, and the wait began once more. Harriet mustered a grim smile. It was the best she could do to reassure her children, but they were old enough to know the truth.

In fact, they celebrated Lizzie's eighth birthday that year. Eight. Harriet whispered a prayer every night asking God to continue watching over them. She had nightmares that Mr. Sanford would sell the girls away in retaliation for the Scott's lawsuit.

The U. S. Supreme Court heard Dred's case over the course of a week in February 1856. Unable to come to a decision, they ordered reargument for the next year and adjourned before the summer heat hit the capital.

But before the heat of summer arrived, Dred, now sixty-two, became ill with tuberculosis. Harriet took care of him as best she could, but everyone knew this illness would take him. Eliza and Lizzie, still officially in hiding with Milly, brought their parents food and news.

"The St. Louis newspapers are writing about our case. You're famous, Papa." Eliza reached to open the worn curtains, letting some light into the dark sickroom.

Dred managed a weak smile.

Harriet closed the curtains, trying to block the outside world so her husband could heal.

"I helped Milly today with a new customer," Lizzie said. She sat on her father's bed and held his hand.

"You didn't go to the river?" Harriet said, heart in her throat.

"No, Mama. She's giving me sewing to do in my room." Lizzie had been well taught. She never mentioned aloud where she and Eliza were staying, even though her parents knew.

Dred recovered enough by the fall to take a job sweeping the lawyer's office. In December, just as the Supreme Court began to hear the case again, Mr. Sanford, Mrs. Emerson's brother, suffered a nervous breakdown.

Harriet heard the news as gossip from the women at the river. She returned home and dropped into a kitchen chair, exhausted from the physical demands of the day and the emotional turmoil of the complicated never-ending lawsuits.

Dred trudged in, shoulders slumped. He'd aged greatly since his illness. Harriet was too tired to greet him. He joined her at the table. For a few minutes, they enjoyed the companionable silence.

"The lawyer says the newspapers are running daily stories about our case," Dred said. "Every day they report everything that is said. Apparently everyone in town has an opinion."

"I wish we could find the ones who support us and get them on the jury," Harriet said. She reached for Dred's hand and held it in both of hers.

By the end of January 1857, the newspapers reported that Dred would lose his case. Three months later, the Court issued its written decision. On March sixth, 1857, the Supreme Court ruled that the Missouri Compromise was unconstitutional. The law that was the basis of Dred's case was overturned. No free territory existed, so Dred's argument about living in such a place was moot. Even worse, the Court declared that since Dred and Harriet had been born slaves, they could never be citizens of the

United States. Therefore, they could not use the federal courts to gain their freedom. Once more, Harriet straightened her back and lifted her chin, putting on as positive a face as she could for public view.

Newspapers clamored for Dred's attention. People recognized him on the street. By speaking to reporters, he spared Harriet similar attention. They never revealed where Eliza and Lizzie were hiding, even when Mrs. Emerson—now Mrs. Chaffee—hired a policeman to hunt them down, knowing they must be somewhere in St. Louis.

At another of their kitchen table discussions, Dred told Harriet, "Our 'owner's' new husband, Mr. Chaffee, is an abolitionist." His eyes sparkled with humor.

Harriet shook her head, unable to appreciate the irony. "So now what?"

"The esteemed Mr. Chaffee is a congressman from Massachusetts, and it doesn't look good for him to own people. He plans to sell us to the Blow family, who will free us."

"That will irritate his wife," Harriet said. She pictured the woman she'd known as Mrs. Emerson defending her slave-owner views to her abolitionist husband.

The Blow family, still staunch supporters of Dred's case, did indeed buy the entire family and set them free.

When Dred and Harriet appeared in their lawyer's office to sign their freedom papers with their marks, the lawyer said, "Mr. Chaffee was embarrassed to be associated with this case, but his wife's attorney will go to court to collect the wages you both earned during the trial."

Harriet shook her head. "She never changes. It doesn't matter now. We are free and have the papers to prove it."

A year later, Dred, now sixty-five, lay on his deathbed, finally claimed by tuberculosis. Harriet held his hand, willing her strength into his frail body. How unfair to spend eleven years suing for freedom only to have one year to enjoy it. "Eliza and Lizzie will be here soon, Dred."

A flicker of a smile lit his gaunt face, but his eyes remained closed. He doted on his daughters, both strong young women now.

"You are my strength," Harriet told him. "Together we beat Mrs. Emerson and Mrs. Russell and Colonel Sanford. More importantly, we ensured our daughters' future. Any children they have will be born free. And on our future grandchildren's eighth birthdays, I will bake a cake and buy them new clothes." She squeezed his hand, which lay limply in hers.

Eliza and Lizzie arrived to see their mother holding their father's hand with tears streaming down her face.

Some say when a person dies, loved ones can see their soul departing the body. Some say the person just falls asleep. Either way, Dred's body and soul were finally free.

Author's Note

Although several previous cases in Missouri had resulted in freedom for enslaved people, the Dred Scott case, decided in 1857, came at a politically sensitive time in United States history as political divisions over slavery intensified and the country headed for Civil War. The Dred Scott decision declared the Missouri Compromise, which prohibited slavery in some territories, unconstitutional. It also deepened the conflict between North and South by allowing enslaved people to be taken anywhere as property, free territory or not, and it stated that African Americans were not citizens. This meant they could not use the courts to sue for their freedom.

After eleven years of litigation, the Scotts lost their lawsuit. They were turned over to Dred's original enslavers, the Blow family, who freed them two months after the decision. Dred died a year later. It is not known if her daughter's age was actually what catapulted Harriet to sue for freedom at that time, but it surely was a factor. Harriet lived for eighteen years after the decision, continuing to do laundry while she enjoyed her daughters and grandchildren.

For a personal look at Dred and Harriet's early years together, read *The River Remembers*, a novel by Linda Ulleseit.

THE STORM

BY ANNE M. BEGGS

PART ONE

March, 1199 AD

Sir Geoffrey observed the small dining hall of the inn in the midmorning light. King Richard laughed and enjoyed the merriment with his soldiers and advisors. It felt good to get out of the siege encampment, to sit on a bench at a table and imbibe the wine with them all. Yet something nagged at him; he felt a dark cloud of doubt. While everyone enjoyed this fine moment on a spring day, his contrary nature caused him to question the comfort. As the king's shield, he could never let his guard down, especially when the king was full of himself and on the prowl for mischief.

Oh, illustrious king, ruler of us all, anointed by God: "By God and my right," the king often said. Geoffrey knew the truth of that proclamation, watching the smiles and good humor surrounding him.

"The walls will crumble," Mercadior, one of King Richard's chief captains, said to more cheers.

"And those we don't throw from the ramparts will hang," said another of the king's men, to even more jeering.

Geoffrey held up his cup in continued tribute to yesterday's stunning assault upon Châlus-Cabrol. The rebellious lord of the castle had pleaded for peace, an end to the siege, and begged for mercy for his people, to which Geoffrey's own Lion-Hearted king decreed there would be no mercy and no prisoners.

Let them stew in their fear and regret. Tomorrow would see the end of them all, Geoffrey thought with deep satisfaction. He was the shield to the greatest of all kings.

"Storm," his friend Henry said. Storm was one of Geoffrey's nicknames, capturing his dark, brooding, volatile nature and his thundering prowess in battle. "*Prosit,* man, cheer up. You are somber in this celebratory moment. Gloomy in the joyous moments, smiling in the darkest ones. Contrary, always."

"This battle is not won, and it is imprudent to assume victory," Geoffrey said to his friend. "The true fight awaits, and I can taste it."

"Correct again, Storm. Yet," Henry said, taking his arm, "I wonder at your courage, your heart. You are bravest in battle. Death holds no fear for you. But I think, mayhap, it is living you fear. Face life with equal boldness."

Geoffrey shook off Henry's hold with a stern glare.

"I hope I am wrong, my friend," Henry said under his breath.

The outer door of the inn opened, and Geoffrey stood to see who entered. Two women, who appeared harmless enough. Yet, the king was in a mood, and females of any sort might bring trouble.

"Storm," a knight said to him, "do you think those women are a threat to the king?"

"Not to my eyes," Geoffrey said with a nod as he approached

them. Their female curves, adorned with finer garments than the camp attendants, were a delight after so much time in battle.

"These are dangerous times, ladies, yet you are unescorted," Geoffrey said.

The brown-haired woman met his gaze with brazen assurance. The other, blonde, wouldn't meet his gaze but swallowed and stared at her feet.

"As our escort has been seduced into service to our great king over there," the brown-haired woman said, turning her dark eyes toward the king, "we were on our own to seek solace in the chapel before returning here to our room. I am Lady Alais." Another brazen act, to introduce herself by her given name, not her husband's. *The king might enjoy her,* he thought, grinning in acknowledgment—"And this is my cousin, Maid Melangell. Our escort, her brother, Sir Louis, brought us here to meet with her betrothed, but this siege has postponed the husband-to-be. All travel has ceased."

"Seduced, is it?" he said with a chuckle. "Do you agree?" he asked the quaking maid, still looking down, wringing—no, choking—a linen scarf in her anxious hands; pink ribbons adorned her hair, woven into two small braids, one braid had fallen over her right shoulder, with her hanging tresses. What were their true loyalties? To King Philip of France or King Richard? Were they genuinely two abandoned women trapped in this inn?

"This siege has brought all travel to a halt, and here we wait. While Louis plays soldier—I mean, serves our king as is his function," Alais said, gazing towards the king and the jovial men surrounding him.

"You are fortunate to be in this inn, rather than on the road. No safer place, at least this day," he said with a wink, though the blonde-haired maiden didn't see it.

"And who are you, good sir?" Alais asked him.

Geoffrey smiled, preparing to answer.

"He is the Storm," Henry said, joining them. "Don't let those sun-gold curls and glowing cheeks fool you. He is a black cloud of gloom and vengeance in the king's service."

"He speaks truth, ladies. I am a storm that none can weather. You have been warned."

Melangell looked up, as if believing a storm would unfold, dropping her scarf. Her blue eyes blinked in trepidation. *Had he pushed her to tears? Poor child.*

"Who are you really, sir?" Melangell asked. Her voice was meek and cracking, yet bold with language. How was this possible? Perhaps bold because she forced herself to speak at all.

"Sir Geoffrey. The Storm. The king's shield, always," he said, retrieving her scarf from the ground.

Placing it in her hands, he introduced Henry. "Shall I escort you tender lambs to your chambers?" Henry asked. "The stairs are perilous."

"We are in peril, sir, but not of the stairs. Usually, I would be most appreciative," Alais said, "but I am responsible for my cousin in this moment." She sighed, glancing at Melangell, "and regretfully decline."

This woman did have her sights on the king, and was that a bad thing? If both were willing, why not, Geoffrey thought, watching her glances between him, Henry, and the king?

"I would ease your burden," Henry said.

"Stop," Geoffrey said, giving Henry a shove. "No time for a dalliance." Alais had her sights on the king. He and Henry must return to duty before King Richard got himself in trouble with this vixen. The king was confident and in full rut, feeling his own sense of victory and invincibility on this beautiful day. Geoffrey felt his own lust rising.

"Henry, leave it," he said, seeing Henry taking the maid's elbow, attempting to escort her to the stairs. Mischief indeed.

Best both these troublemakers were upstairs and barricaded from them all. What a sweetling Melangell was; could it be she smiled at him?

"Go on," he said to Henry, who pretended to drool in exaggerated appreciation of the women before him, then blew kisses to them both. "Ladies," Geoffrey said to them, "please, you are bait, teasing a pack of wolves," he continued, pointing to the stairs, indicating they go.

"You are quite the shield, sir," Alais said, "though you deny your king his due," she continued, running her tongue over her upper lip.

"Wolves and vixens, a deadly pairing," he said, reaching for her elbow to push her towards the stairs, knowing Melangell would follow. "Take your cousin upstairs at least. She deserves better."

"Mellie, how do you thank Sir Geoffrey for his kindness, his service to you?" Alais asked, shoving Melangell towards him.

Her eyes widened as she stared back and forth between Alais and him.

"He retrieved your scarf and shields you from his friends," Alais said, though her tone was sarcastic.

"Thank you, sir. You do our king great service," she whispered.

"Show your appreciation! Are you not to give him your scarf?" Alais snapped, pushing her closer.

"Unnecessary, Maiden. Run upstairs and lock the door before your wicked cousin causes you more embarrassment," Geoffrey said, smirking towards the wayward Alais.

Melangell ran. But Geoffrey had seen the blush upon her cheeks. Sweetling indeed. Alais sauntered behind her, glancing back over her shoulder.

Returning to the table, Henry and he met with laughs and joking.

"I thought for sure, Storm, you would bring that fair and lascivious lady to me. Her intentions were plain enough," the king said.

"Lady Alais, the brown-haired one. Shall I retrieve her?"

"Let the partridge baste in her anticipation, as I savor the thought. It is good to be here," he said, looking about the table. "This land is my treasure."

"To your long reign as the King of England, Aquitaine, France, and beyond, Your Grace," Geoffrey said. "I am grateful to share this glorious campaign with you, always."

As if summoned, Lady Alais returned, pink ribbons in hand. "Your Grace," she said to King Richard with a deep curtsy, "if I might have a word with the Storm." She smiled at him, as if he, and not the king, was her intended.

"The Storm?" men asked and chuckled. It was the king she wanted, wasn't it?

The king nodded, amused.

"On reflection, Maid Melangell does wish to thank her champion and bestow these, her ribbons, to you."

Ribald teasing erupted around the table.

He took the ribbons—soft silken pink, rich colors of hidden promise. It was wrong to keep these under false pretense; he must return them later.

"Storm! Would you turn down a maid's request?" the king said, laughing as his men did.

"What request?" Geoffrey asked.

"Those ribbons are an intimate thing indeed. You must see to her."

"I am your shield, not hers. Today I ride with you."

"Plenty of time to ride, sir," the king said to more laughs. "You must see to the woman's needs. Today it is my command." Alais was already seated next to King Richard, both with cups in their hands. In full rut.

Reluctantly, Geoffrey climbed the creaking stairs. His duty was to his king and the king said attend. Going down the hall, he knocked on the closed doors, asking if Maid Melangell was there. On the third door, rather than a firm 'no,' he heard a gasp. It resounded in his chest as an invitation.

She opened the door; he entered.

"Maid Melangell, your request for my return was honored by our king. He commanded I see to your needs, and perhaps my own." He smiled.

She wilted. "I—my request?"

"You sent your ribbons. An intimate invitation that I return to your side," he said, holding them up.

She studied the ribbons, touched her hair, her neck. Her hair was loose and hung in mead-colored splendor, highlighted by the blush of her cheeks. Were she to smile, he knew it would be radiant. She stiffened.

"Alais! She demanded those ribbons, claiming urgency and need. That her appearance was lacking." Melangell stepped into the hallway. "Where has everyone gone? We are alone."

There was no one in the hallway, but the raucous noise below indicated a full room and seemed to chase her back into her chamber. Prudent girl. Or was she? Her cousin was eager to court danger below and had left bewildered Melangell to him. Why?

"You did not send these? The king and I were deceived? Well, this is a surprise." He could have assuaged her alarm and embarrassment, but she became more alluring in her modesty. "It appears your cousin is a scheming woman and has abandoned you as your brother did."

Her cousin set her up, to his advantage. How could he repay the devious Lady Alais? This was a favor indeed. No, the maid awaited her betrothed. Was she a gift the king could so impulsively give to him? Yes. No. "Thus, I must return these to you. I would not hold them in false admiration." *Storm*, he reminded himself, *you did come to return them.*

She looked down, then at the ribbons, and then up to his disappointed expression. He hoped he looked disappointed. "They are a mere echo of what might have been between us," he said with a sigh. With his gauntlets tucked into his girdle, he held the ribbons out upon his open palm, his calloused hand stained with dirt and blood that no amount of scrubbing seemed able to remove, and so it should be.

"I—I do admire you, sir. That is not deceit. But—I—it isn't done this way. Not a maid being so bold." Yet she did not take the offered ribbons. Rather she stared at them, then back at him. The edges of her mouth quivering, beads of sweat on her upper lip. A delicious lip, begging a kiss. Why else would she remain against her own words? Bold and modest at once. What a brew of desire she presented.

"Precious maiden, I must—" he inhaled, letting his breath out with a groan. Then another sigh. Did he imagine it, or did she truly smell of roses and lavender, and the heavenly aroma only a woman possessed? The delicate pink ribbons represented all she was. "I must warn you. I would be remiss."

She waited in silence.

"You are the temptress," he said, caressing her hair, her cheek, as she pressed into his hand. "But I am the tempest. The storm you cannot weather. You crave protection, little doe, yet court the wolf."

She shuddered. Was she to spring away as a clever doe must?

"Whether you realize it or not, these ribbons bind us, as our king proclaims," he murmured, placing one in her hand, wrapping the other around her neck, drawing her close to him. "Are you to stand on your two feet for our first kiss, or am I to hold you up?"

She said nothing but tried to stand tall.

"Toe to toe," he said, bending to kiss her, to devour her as she surrendered herself to him. As King Richard had suspected. Oh, splendid, generous king, wise in the needs of a woman.

Their kiss was slow and tantalizing.

"Wise are the ways of our king," he murmured, "bringing us together."

He should not. Yet this sweetling was a gift from their king. He must not. Such a sweetling she was, her mouth, her scent. She was seeking another kiss, his mouth moving to her neck. Her ... No, he thought to pull away.

"You are a feast. A banquet. This humble servant of the king is undeserving of your delicate bounty," he said, stepping back, still holding her up. God's eyes, he came to return her ribbons, yet how easily the words of seduction and coercion ambled off his tongue in smooth rhythm. *Return the ribbons. The ribbons.*

One ribbon was still around her damp, kiss-covered neck. He discovered the other around his neck, with no recollection of her placing it there in their passion.

Duty. What was his duty? His hand went to the pink ribbon adorning her neck.

"Pink is my favorite color now," he said, letting his fingers caress her cheek, "or should I say blush? Full bloom. Matched by the—" He paused, closing his eyes, envisioning the pleasures before him. Blushing, promising, female. Saints on a cross, the king wasn't the only one in rut.

She took the ends of the ribbon around his neck and on tiptoes kissed him again. A gift, she was presenting herself willingly.

Doors slammed and feet pounded up the stairs. The king and Alais, he suspected, thankful for the distraction and relief the king was occupied as he and Melangell were.

But no, it was not the king, not his footfall or voice. Geoffrey knew he must leave. His duty was the king.

"You are to marry another," he said hoarsely, not believing his own words. *Go to the door*, he told himself.

"Willingly, I would marry," she said in a whisper, soft as her parted lips. Sitting on the stool, arms out, he invited her to come sit in his lap.

"You are betrothed. A contract between your father and him. I cannot interfere, Maiden. I said you were the temptress, and that is heartbreakingly true. Men like me devour sweetlings like you." Spitting out the bones without a glance back, he reflected with honest brutality...not true, he had never hurt a woman. "Not you and not today. Nor can I guard your door night and day. I pray your betrothed arrives soon." Her brother Louis, had no chance against any of the king's men if they forgot their duty, as they often did, but he wouldn't terrify her with that prospect.

"But we—after what you said and did. The king gave me to you. As husband and wife. You claimed as much," she said, tears forming.

He had said and did much. But they could not wed.

"I am the king's shield. I move and fight as he commands, Maiden. We do not marry."

Her hand went to her mouth as her tears fell, and she shook her head with sorrow. He had spared her, surely. It seemed everyone had sacrificed her to the king, to him. Why, he wondered again?

"You are too trusting. I pray your husband is worthy of you," he said, wondering if such a man existed. "We shared a kiss —" He paused, listening.

Shouts filled the air. All alarmed.

Geoffrey pushed Melangell aside, rushing to the window.

"The king has been shot!"

PART TWO

The day after King Richard was shot in the shoulder by a crossbow, his men took Châlus-Cabrol in avenging glory; Storm's heart pounding in rhythm with his sword, each stroke or thrust took the king closer to his place upon this dais, and in a suitable bedchamber for his recovery.

"No quarter," Storm said, leading his men up the ramparts. "Throw them off," he commanded, chasing the fleeing men, who had surrendered, hoping for mercy.

"At least let us collect their weapons, Storm," Mercadior said with a chuckle. "Fill our coffers, eh?"

"Leave this to others," Henry said. "Let us bring the injured king. This is his victory."

Once the king was ensconced in the castle, Geoffrey never left his king's bedside. Days and nights he held vigil, seeing to the king's needs. Food, drink, stories, and gaiety. Bring a priest. Send the priest away. The king's friends and advisors flooded in and out with Geoffrey's authority.

"It should have been me," Geoffrey moaned to anyone and everyone. "I should never have left his side. That bolt was meant for me. I was his shield. Always his shield."

"Your behavior brings shame upon us all. If you are guilty, we are all guilty. I am not. Even at my post, I could not prevent our Grace's impetuous, invincible belief in himself," Henry said, though Geoffrey knew the knight had wept nearly as much as he had.

"We have a kingdom to protect. We ride soon," said another.

"Storm, you lame, crying turd. We are all his shields. His swords. The king did what he wanted, against most of our protests," Mercadior said, pointing to their bedridden king.

Mercadior was the king's trusted mercenary captain, a

landed knight, and the man walking with the king when he was shot—a God-cursed fool.

"He bid you leave, and you honored his command. Stop this incessant whining, or join a monastery," Mercadior snapped.

Storm he was. Geoffrey jumped to his feet and lunged at Mercadior, bare fists striking.

"This is your fault. To allow such stupidly audacious, unprotected nonsense! What true guard of the king would partake in that foul stunt? To leave the inn, allowing the king, with no armor, no *maille*, to parade defenselessly around the castle. You useless, unthinking, feckless cock of a pig!" Geoffrey shouted, beating the man with his fists, kicking him as he fell.

"Storm!" the king shouted, wasting his waning strength.

Mercadior's men had him back on his feet.

"Draw your sword, lord," one shouted.

"Arm yourself!" shouted another. The crowded bedchamber shook with shouts and movement.

Mercadior put his hand to the grip. He was one of the king's finest soldiers and leaders. Just the name Mercadior caused good soldiers to drop their weapons. It was how he earned his land and rewards.

Storm was faster and stronger. Storms always were. As Storm came in for battle, he saw the look in Mercadior's eyes: fear, defeat, and the desire to live another day. The coward would not fight, would not defend himself against the king's true shield. Not this day. Maybe not any day. And the recognition—a debt now existed between them. Mercadior didn't like it, of course, but the acknowledgement was there. Storm was sure of it.

Just as readily, Mercadior's men stood before their leader, a bulwark of protection against the raging storm. Geoffrey could not defeat them all.

Hours later, there was banging on the door. Geoffrey stood from his place at the king's bed, waiting. The injured king nodded. "Let them enter," he said.

"Enter," Geoffrey said.

Mercadior came first. "The foul crossbowman, Your Grace. For your judgment."

Finally, Geoffrey thought, the lowest miscreant—a cursed crossbowman. Days he had considered fitting punishments to befall this enemy of the realm. He should suffer as their ailing king did. The pain Geoffrey also prayed to assume upon himself. He was the shield.

Two soldiers followed; between them, they held a youth, perhaps a mere boy.

The king indicated Geoffrey help him sit up, bravely shrugging off his agony.

"We have never met. How is it we are enemies?" King Richard asked, his voice firm and assured despite his worsening malady.

"You killed my father and brothers in this siege upon our home. I am bound to avenge my family," the youth said, with greater bravado than a boy of his years should possess. Child or not, his crime was unforgivable. His age compounded Geoffrey's guilt. A damned boy with a crossbow—this should be Geoffrey's fate. God, he asked again, why our magnificent king?

"Indeed," the king said with a slight nod.

What punishment are we both to endure? Geoffrey wondered, waiting.

As if seeking confidence, the boy looked about at all the hostile faces, all waiting for the king's verdict.

"I am to face your full wrath, lord," he said, but his voice weakened. Geoffrey suspected he was succumbing to terror. As the boy trembled, Geoffrey found greater strength. The time had come. His time. Ultimate atonement for not protecting his king. What the boy would suffer, he too would submit himself.

"You know little of the world or my wrath. Would you retract your hasty words?" the king asked the youth, his face impassive, despite the pain of his injury.

"I regret I couldn't save my family."

"Say the word, Your Grace," Mercadior said. "By my hand, it will be done."

Geoffrey inhaled, preparing to assume his position with the prisoner. Both to suffer the king's vengeance and God's.

"You impress me, young man. I respect honor. By my will, I exonerate you."

In fear, the boy hung his head.

"What?" Mercadior said, glaring from the king to the boy.

Others exclaimed the same. What just happened? Exonerate? Did he not mean execute?

"Honesty, courage. I forgive you. You are free from retribution. Mercadior," the king said. "Give the lad some gold coins. Such is my forgiveness."

Geoffrey watched in shocked silence as the weeping boy was led away. What justice was this?

What would bring on this benevolent action, Geoffrey and the king's retainers questioned? What magnificence of forgiveness was King Richard possessed of? *Oh, greatest of kings,* Geoffrey thought. *What lesson could a soldier take from this?*

Geoffrey watched in guilt and horror as the king's flesh went putrid; day by day, the malady spread the poison throughout his body. Visions, nightmares, and pain-induced rants filled the remaining hours of the king's dwindling life.

Melangell's pink ribbon, though small, was a constant reminder of his fault in this, and he tied it tightly around his throat as a painful reminder of his negligence, his guilt.

"Geoffrey!" Henry said in alarm, entering the death chamber. "What are you doing?"

The ribbon was so tight he couldn't answer. He waved his hand, indicating Henry keep his voice down while the king slept.

Henry's eyes were wide as he drew his eating knife. "I'm cutting that off. You're mad!"

Geoffrey tried to push his hand away but relented as Henry cut into his neck to get the choking ribbon off.

"What nonsense is this? God's blood," Henry sighed as the ribbon gave way. "The maid's ribbon? Why?"

"Give it to me," Geoffrey said, reaching for it.

"No."

The friends stared at each other. How could Geoffrey make him understand? Cursed ribbon, if only there was enough of it to hang himself.

"If you love her so much, perhaps we can intervene—" Henry was cut off.

"No. She is betrothed. This is my penance for leaving the king's side," Geoffrey said, his throat dry and raspy.

"You need a priest. Self-slaughter is a sin before God. I have no words for this corruption of your soul."

King Richard snorted, then cried out in his suffering.

"Give me the ribbon. Please," Geoffrey hissed. "I promise no further attempt. Return the token to me."

Standing, he snatched the ribbon from his friend. Then he turned and poured wine for the king. He helped his king sit up to drink, offering the only comfort he could. "Bring a priest, if you must," he said to Henry. "Mayhap he will have solace for our king."

In vain, Geoffrey tried to assume his liege's pain, take on the sickness and untimely death. It was his function to protect the king. If he had only been there. If only he had denied his lust and vanity. "God, why? Why do you let him suffer when it is I who deserve this?"

"Storm," the king called, his voice feeble. Geoffrey held a cup to him. "You and I—my contrary reflection," the king said, taking the cup. "In my moments of darkest despair, you were my shield. A shining star of glory, strength, and belief when I was a prisoner of doubt.

"In my moments of zealous pride and arrogance, when my advisors would bolster my invincibility, you were the black cloud —my storm of doom and prudence, shielding me from my poor judgment and vanity."

"Thank you, Your Grace. It is my honor to protect you," Geoffrey said, his throat constricting with that reflection.

"This day, when I lie in agony, doubt upon me...where is...? I need your shield of light, of glory to come. Yet you wallow in despair and self-imposed suffering, threatening harm to yourself. Let the priest bear the hair shirt in penance. Others can self-flagellate. I need my great Storm," the king said, with a stern, penetrating stare, "to burn away my fear and sorrow. Embrace life, help me."

Geoffrey could think of no greater aid than to suffer, sharing his king's fate.

"Go find your strength. Our purpose," the king whispered, his voice failing, as Geoffrey was failing him.

"I will, Your Grace." With this command, Geoffrey took himself to the chapel outside the castle.

Trudging from the king, he heard the murmurs and taunts from the other men.

"He is mad, possessed of some malady of spirit."

"Every day worse."

"I think Satan haunts him."

"The chapel is the safest place for him. And away from us."

"Storm, it pleases me to see you go to the chapel," Henry said as they passed.

Kneeling before the altar, he felt the hypocrite. The chapel was no place for him, unless the priest helped him hang himself —with the pink ribbon. And where was the priest? *Wretched man, am I. Helpless to protect my king. Useless. I am the feckless one.* Geoffrey's chest heaved, his lungs barely drew breath with the weight of his grief, yet there was not enough weight to crush him. He too lingered, as his king.

"God, please, each hour I beseech you. Let me trade my life for my king's. He is Your greater servant. He has Your work yet to do. I am unworthy, my king sent me here for guidance. To pray. To find my way, and his."

He bent his head in sublimation. In the hope God or a saint might behead him. What dark unholy thoughts he held in a house of God. Was he haunted by Satan? The final storm he could not weather?

He heard the faintest footsteps. *Please, let this be the end.*

Someone knelt next to him. He smelled lavender; paradise between a woman's...arms...he amended, remembering he was in a chapel, seeking God's favor. Pink ribbons. Melangell. Heaven.

He hesitated. *Should he speak? Did she wish to break the silence?* In the whole inside of the chapel, she chose to kneel next to him, demanding attention—offering diversion.

"Maid Melangell," he said, deciding to speak first if he wanted to control the dialogue. "These are very hard days for us all. What brings you to the chapel?"

"These are the hardest days, sir. I hear you suffer greatly, in agony with our king. I come to pray for his and your health and safety, sir. There is much between us. Much that binds us," she said.

He studied her. Though kneeling, she was strong and sure in her place within the chapel, within God's world. One of the pink ribbons was still tied with a sweet bow around her neck.

"You still wear your ribbon, though it is tight enough to choke you, sir. Is that your true intent?" Melangell asked.

It was. He needed this constant, painful reminder of his great shame, his dereliction of duty to the king. But for these ribbons...

"It reminds me of our king's suffering and my absence when he needed me most."

"Perhaps I too must tighten my ribbon. I would not see you suffer alone."

He put his hand on hers, shaking his head. "I beg you, no. I would not see you suffer, too."

She had the glimmer of a smile. An acceptance of his request. And relief, surely.

"You blame yourself, yet you, we, did the king's bidding."

The echo of her sweet voice caused a ripple across his skin. Nearly causing him to forget his guilt. They had kissed. He had nuzzled her superb neck, soft and flowing with life. What strength he possessed that day, to walk away before the temptation was too great.

"I sinned. Forsook my king," he said, bringing himself back.

"We did as commanded."

She reached up and touched the choking ribbon on his neck.

"These ribbons are tokens of our love, and our king's will," she said. "Mayhap to lives yet to be born in service to our kin."

Tokens of love or reminders of guilt, he reflected, as deadly as a bolt from a crossbow.

PART THREE

April 6, 1199 AD

Nine days later, the warm sun mocked the horror of the day. Never could anyone remember so much grief and mourning when King Richard the Lion-Hearted, great Pilgrimage King, defender of the Holy Land, Ruler by God and his right died ten days after being shot by a crossbow. Dastardly, dastardly deed. Chaos erupted.

The king died without a named, legal heir. His kingdom was still at war with rebellious factions in Aquitaine and beyond. Was his young and untested brother, John Lackland, to be crowned king of all this? What turmoil was upon them?

"Bring the man forth," Mercadior ordered. "He will suffer the fate he chose."

Despite King Richard's orders that the youth be freed, Mercadior had imprisoned the crossbowman just in case the king didn't survive. No one kills a king and goes free. No one.

"You would defy our king's orders," Geoffrey shouted in defiance. "His last great act of benevolence is to be reversed by a worthless coward like you?"

"Take him away, before he too suffers the same fate!" Mercadior called.

"Take me! I should be flailed in his place," Geoffrey said, having heard the men murmur that penalty. "It is our fault the king died," Geoffrey said, already assuming a position next to the prisoner. This day, he would follow his king. His suffering, too, would end this day. Before all. This was devotion to duty. This was love for a king.

"You assume too much, Storm. You are weak with grief and malady of spirit. You will not die at my hand. Mayhap the priesthood is calling you," Mercadior said.

Henry moved to Geoffrey's side.

"Greater than the priesthood, where is your loyalty to our beloved king's realm, his family, his kingdom? Who is to guard his sacred journeys to final rest?" Henry asked, continuing when Geoffrey stood mute. "The king's entrails will be buried here, near Châlus-Chabrol. He wished to have his body buried with his father, Henry, in Fontevraud Abbey. As you know, his heart —the heart of the lion—goes to Rouen. All require a large, armed retinue. Which are you to attend, Storm?" Henry asked.

Which indeed. Geoffrey's mind spun with all this. Where would he best serve his king? Mind, body, soul, at rest. Permanent rest on this war-torn ground, while the king's soul was in God's paradise. The king should have told him what to do, where to go, how best to continue serving him. Geoffrey planned battles, led men in the fighting. In this he was clever, educated and strong. He followed orders and gave them to great success.

Now he was without his king's guidance. Richard had abandoned them. He must be strong, showing men what needed to be done, which actions to take. They were still at war, the kingdom at risk. He was still the king's and the realm's shield.

In the following days, there was more unrest.

"The inn burns!" Henry shouted.

"The fools," Geoffrey said, seeing some of their own men taking more vengeance upon the town. "Stop! Would you destroy your king's property, his kingdom?"

Terrified townspeople threw buckets of water upon their properties to keep the fire from spreading.

"Help them, or before God I will throw you upon the flames," Geoffrey shouted.

Melangell was outside crying. "My cousin Alais is still inside."

"Where? Lady Alais!" he called, circling the inn, already assessing the building was lost.

"Help!" She was at an upstairs window, flames all around her, black smoke pouring out around her, concealing her for a moment.

"Jump!" he shouted, running to the flaming building, as close as he dared. Arms outstretched. Her face, blackened by soot, was barely visible. "Jump, you heathen bitch, or let Satan take you! I'll come no closer."

"Jump!" Melangell shouted.

His men were there, all imploring her to jump. She did, missing Geoffrey and knocking Henry down with the impact.

"Get them to the castle," Geoffrey said to Henry, already pushing Melangell to him. "I'll manage this."

Again, he took charge, directing and disciplining the factions of the king's men and the townspeople.

"Before God, Storm, I had my doubts," Mercadior said with a mean smile, and a mouth with half his teeth missing. "Supporting me, my decisions, despite our unfinished business. The men followed you, thus following me with more loyalty than I might have garnered myself. You were the man, the shield, our King Richard always believed in.

"That said, you must decide. The king's heart leaves tomorrow and the body in a day. Which will you escort? The heart to Rouen or the body to Fontevraud? I give you first choice, Storm. I will escort the other."

"Lord Mercadior, you do me great honor with your high praise and generous offer," Geoffrey said with a nod. "There is no space in this dire time for our feuds and hostilities. I continue to bow to your leadership and will make no treasonous arrangements behind your back."

Geoffrey fought to control the building storm of his own indecision. It was as if he were being pulled apart by three horses in three different directions. He could not be all places at once as the remains of King Richard could. To Fontevraud with the remaining body, to Rouen with the heart, or remain here with the entrails—saddest of locations, this place of the king's death. He felt tremors building within him. *Not now, not before Mercadior. Not before the men.* The mercenary Mercadior was the best they had. He and Mercadior studied each other in a brief and silent moment.

"You must decide," Mercadior insisted.

"I will let you know by sundown, if not sooner. Thank you again, lord."

"I will instruct both groups to start packing," Mercadior said with a scowl.

Henry joined him as he fled to the chapel one more time. Another chance to find redemption and guidance. "You're shaking, Storm. Are you truly ill this time?"

Geoffrey shook his head.

"Most of us wagered you would ride with the heart of our lion. But others wonder if Maid Melangell holds greater sway on you."

Melangell. Is this what held him rooted in the foul town of King Richard's murder? What fate had pushed them together—stars, spirits, God and king? What was he to do with a woman? She couldn't travel with him. Couldn't go where he would need to go. This storm was unfathomable, even for him. All was bleak and he felt the rage of uncertainty within.

"Are you to join me in prayer?" Geoffrey asked his friend.

"If you need me, of course, otherwise I pack for travel."

"You pack. I will pray." Again, he entered the chapel. Several candles burned on the altar and Melangell was there, kneeling. His loud footsteps roused her from her prayers, and she stood in welcome.

"Greetings. I am glad to see you this day," she said. "I must thank you again for saving Alais and me."

"Henry saved the Lady Alais."

"He took your lead. You sent us to the castle."

He nodded.

"I hear you will be leaving us soon with his remains."

"Perhaps," he said.

She lowered her head. "I believed. Or hoped. I thought—"

Another long pause as she searched the confined chapel. She placed her hand to the pink ribbon still tied with delicate care around her neck, glancing up to see his was still tightly around his. What words did he have? Was this another storm or a calming breeze? It was both.

"These are uncertain times. Dangerous times," she said, brushing away a lingering tear. Was it the candlelight reflecting upon her soft, rosy complexion? Even without a smile, she was radiant. Glowing in God's light and strength. "You have purpose, still. I only wish I were part of it."

What understanding. Such eloquence for one so young and inexperienced. How many females were like this? Had he been so negligent to see the purer value in them?

"Your silence speaks for you," she said. "Yet, the ribbon remains."

His mind had been a violent torrent of thoughts and feelings. Had he been mute all this time? The clouds burned away in her light; the melody of her voice stilled the pounding in his head. He would hear more.

"Your words speak deeply. I have felt no clarity in days." It was true. He had been adrift in grief and anger, unable to find respite. Again, this girl, this young woman of vitality and innocence, wisdom in youth, guided him. "I dare not utter your name, lest I wake from this dream and fall back into the nightmare."

She burst with life. What power she wielded against his storm. Was Henry right? Was he fearless in the face of death, because he was afraid to live? Melangell was life.

And he did have purpose and understood now how he must execute it. "Beautiful, radiant child of God. I am unworthy of your grace. You have opened my eyes and my heart. I will make it right between us in this world, fairest of ladies. Favored by God and the Host, you have shown me the way."

He took both her hands in his, laying kisses and tears upon them. To ask more of her in this tenderest and most grateful of moments would corrupt it. Again, she had given her all. Could he do any less?

He left her in the chapel. Striding to the stable, he felt buoyant. His path was clear before him, but he had much to do.

Geoffrey reread his letter before signing it:

Lady Melangell,
I haven't enough time. You showed me the way, the truth,
my duty. I sold all I possessed in this mortal life—I will
not need them. You were correct. Our King did proclaim
our union. I honor you as my Lady Wife, and as my
widow. Take this money, meager as it is, to fund a new
life. Lord Mercadior will see to it. Trust him as I do.
God's light and life shines within you. You are of His
world, courageous enough to live. With the heart of a
lioness, I think. I am forever grateful for your wisdom, for
setting me on my true path. I am the king's shield always
and will protect his soul though I know he is welcomed to
Heaven by God, our Savior Jesus, and the saints. He needs
me still. I know this. I follow the light. The Brightest
Light. The storm is at rest.
Geoffrey

"What do you mean you sold your horse?" Henry asked, incredulously.

"I don't need a horse to escort my king. I shall walk at his side. As I should have done so in life," Geoffrey said, unable to contain his smile.

"You have joined a priesthood, haven't you?" Henry asked, hurt, still unbelieving.

Mercadior was even less amused on hearing the great and thunderous Storm had sold most of his gear and horse. "Your gleefulness in walking as a peasant alongside our king speaks in greater urgency to your madness, Storm. You will be an insult. And slow them down. What blight is this?" he snarled.

"No insult, and no treachery in your wake, lord. I have never been surer of my motives," Geoffrey said with a nod.

"Are you bewitched by the maid, or more likely her wicked, singed cousin?" he asked.

"Neither. We understand each other. I would ask you to deliver this to the Maid Melangell in the morning," Geoffrey said, handing Mercadior the letter and a bag of coins. Geoffrey saw the resentful spark of recognition in the brute's eyes. The debt would be paid.

"Even ruthless mercenaries have a sense of honor," Geoffrey said with a deeper bow. He could count on Mercadior. "This letter is for you. Honor me by reading it on the morrow."

"You won't say it to my face. Who is the coward?" Mercadior said, spitting.

"I am not a coward, but you and Henry would stand in my way. I know my course, my duty. My king calls." He left.

His message to Mercadior requested that he deliver the letter and the money to the Maid Melangell the following morning, and that Mercadior was responsible for finding her a husband or settling her as a bride of Christ, her choice.

"Where are you off to now?" Henry asked, as Geoffrey passed him.

"I am reborn. This requires baptism. At the pond," Geoffrey said, resisting the urge to jog to the beckoning water of renewal, still feeling that he was floating, rather than walking.

Clad only in his linen undershirt and the pink ribbon at his neck, Geoffrey stared into the pond water. Usually dark and threatening to a man who couldn't swim, this night it welcomed him with sweet release. Redemption. Letters were written, explaining himself. Tomorrow they would know he had joined Richard. Yes, Richard, for in heaven there was but one King: God. This was his atonement, his baptism to enter the true Kingdom. Such peace. Never had he felt abundant tranquility; no storm raged. All his life he had been at war with himself.

"Storm!" Henry called

"Sir Geoffrey! Is that you?" Melangell called as well.

Jesus Christ and bleeding saints on a cross, what the hell were they doing here, he thought in frustration.

"You are not dressed!" she said, turning from him, collapsing in a heap, sobbing. Not leaving.

"What? Why?" Henry sputtered. They were both clambering at him with their voices, yapping and crying.

Thundering damn! They disturbed his peace, as he stared at the placid water, that which offered freedom.

"Why are you here?" he asked with exasperation.

"Mercadior sent us," Henry said.

"I read your letter. These coins. No!" Melangell said.

Mercadior, you traitorous bastard, he thought. *Betraying my trust and request.*

"I will not be your widow," she said. "Sir, please."

"We need you! England needs you. Hell, Mercadior admits he needs you." Henry's voice droned on about need and duty; the men unable to lose another leader.

Stepping into the pond, Geoffrey felt the liquid encircle his ankles. Blessed water. He held up a hand to silence their protests. The incessant noise.

"Quiet," he said. "I am—" But his own voice corrupted the silence. *I am in communion. They won't understand.* He felt the light, the cool water. Most of his life he had been at war, storming. Now he found rest. The promise of eternal peace enticed him. His God, Richard: there were no words, just light.

Yet the storm began building dark flames anew; its own ghastly light. This gloomy light he knew intimately—juxtaposed against the tantalizing new radiance. He took another step, deeper. The mud oozed between his toes, a glorious memory of boyhood, a simple delight when he didn't need to face his mortality.

We need you, they called from the shore. But Paradise

awaited, the gates were open, he need only follow the bright light, but his feet were held in the firmament.

"Sir Geoffrey!" Lady Melangell's shrill voice disrupted the moment.

"Before God, Storm! We must go to Rouen."

His heart thumped, his beating heart. Not a dead one in a box. Inhaling he felt the pink ribbon tighten around his throat. Once a shackle of guilt, now it tethered him to duty, to life. His own battles remained; the storm was yet required. Unsure, he turned to Henry and his lady.

"Let us escort the heart to Rouen."

Author's Note

What small thing could disrupt the reign of a mighty medieval king? What impact would that have upon his kingdom? King Richard was shot by a crossbow and died ten days later. Those last ten days are shrouded in legend and near mythology, as anyone researching the monarch will discover.

Sir Geoffrey is fictional, allowing me to explore the mental anguish of a devoted soldier momentarily distracted by a gift of a simple, pink ribbon. Geoffrey's days are filled with "If only," and self-loathing as he navigates life without the Lion Hearted.

Mercadior is on the historic record. History is a bit dubious about the crossbowman, so I chose what fit my story.

We will never know what possessed King Richard to walk unprotected as he did, mayhap something as small as a ribbon or a dalliance, and that left an echo that reverberated through Europe.

A NOT SO STILL LIFE, WITH APPLES

BY KATHRYN PRITCHETT

Aix-en-Provence
1852

The big wild boy with a tender heart would be hard to reach. She'd need to use something of this earth. Solid, familiar, desirable. It seemed a cliche to employ Eve's tool, the same one that lured Adam into greater knowledge. But what better object of desire than the first one? She lifted her veil to set up her stall in the village square and laid out the apples—red with hints of gold, elegant chartreuse stars glittering near the stems.

She hurried to complete her task before the other boy—a slight, fatherless child—reached her stall. This urchin would be her conduit to the wild boy. "Apples for sale, apples!" she cried in his direction.

He stumbled up to her stall dragging a worn, empty basket. The day before he'd been rescued from some schoolyard bullies by the older, wealthier wild boy, and he still bore a hunted look. He carefully looked around, before staring longingly at the fragrant orbs.

"Would you like some?" she said, ignoring the crick in her knees as she reached towards him. "Only a sou for the whole lot."

The urchin set his empty basket on the ground and pulled out the linings of his pockets. "Don't have even a centime."

"Ah, that's too bad," she said, not wanting to frighten him away. "Anything else you can offer in exchange?"

The boy squinted up at the sky. "I can tell you a story," he said at last, smiling broadly.

"And what good is a story?" she countered.

His face fell briefly, but he puffed out his scrawny chest and replied, "A story can feed the soul."

She laughed at his audacity. "All right, you feed my soul, and I'll feed your belly."

The boy commenced with a tale about a rascally pig who rambled through a series of improbable adventures. The veiled woman clapped her hands.

"That's quite the tale," she said, patting her belly. "I do indeed feel fed by it. So much so, I will give you all my apples. Perhaps you'll find a friend to share them with, Monsieur…"

"Z-zola," said the boy, warily. "Émile Zola."

"Very well, Monsieur Zola, on your way now." She handed him the full basket, hoping the seed she'd planted about sharing his bounty with a friend would immediately bear fruit.

After he'd skipped out of the square, the woman quickly followed him to 28 rue de l'Opéra and waited in the shadow of an imposing chestnut tree, drawing her dark shawl up to her eyes. She saw him approach the banker's fine stone house obliquely, still scanning the street for any trouble. He paused on the doorstep before rapping the large knocker that summoned a maidservant. "Yes?" she inquired.

"Is the young master at home?" He bowed his head.

The girl turned and called inside, "Monsieur Paul!"

A few moments later, the glowering wild child pushed past her and scowled at the younger boy. Émile thrust the basket of apples at him. "Merci Paul," he cried. "You saved me yesterday and in return I have brought you these."

A rare mix of astonishment and delight replaced the wild boy's stormy visage. He shook his unruly curls before accepting the basket and retreating into the shadow of his father's grand home.

"Come back!" cried Émile.

She held her breath as they both stared at the dark entrance.

Before long Paul returned to the light and motioned for the younger boy to follow him. "All right then. Come in, Émile, come in."

The Picnic, 1869

The wild child who could name every rock in the cliffs surrounding Aix-en-Provence had become a lost man in Paris. The year before when he'd been languishing at his father's fine home, he'd taken courage from Émile's letters that made relocating look so easy. Émile had left their small southern city and almost immediately found a market for his short stories and essays.

In Paris, everything's for sale: wise virgins, foolish virgins, truth and lies, tears and smiles, he'd written.

Paul read these words and believed he could reject his father's insistence that he enter the law. Instead, he would become a painter—though he was only then learning to paint—and the Salon would accept him with open arms. He would thrive as Emile had in the city of dreams.

But the Salon had not embraced the dark fantasies in his art the way the public clamored for Émile's naturalistic stories. Paul's paintings were derided, his company declined. He wandered the streets looking for solace with interchangeable trollops who indulged his insistence on minimal touch.

On a cloudy day much like any other in a Paris winter, Paul searched for hope in a more reputable setting as he made his way to the Académie Suisse. Not that he was in the mood to engage with anyone, but at least he could get out of the cold.

A tall young woman chattered with a friend on a bench in the courtyard, her oval face and almond eyes cocked towards the sky. She paused momentarily to lift an apple, red and gold, to her lips. Just as she bit into the sweet white flesh, a ray of sun broke through the clouds and illuminated the same burnished hues in her dark, upswept hair.

Dazzled by the parallel shades found in the fruit and the girl's coiffure, Paul momentarily stopped his fretting and thought about how he could repeat those colors on a canvas. He'd mix cadmium red and a small hint of blue with a touch of white to mirror the colors revealed in her raven locks. The flecks of gold would be tinted with chartreuse to evoke the hidden star by the apple's stem. After his recent experiments painting with a palette knife, he might return to his brushes. To capture what he saw in her would take fine work.

She was pleasing to look at. Perhaps she was a model by profession and wouldn't be shocked to have a stranger ask to paint her. He brushed by an old, veiled woman to intercept the apple-eater as she rose to walk elsewhere.

"Mademoiselle," he cried. The girl turned, the half-eaten apple still in her hand.

"Yes?"

He bowed his head. "I would like to paint you."

She crossed her arms and gave him a serious appraisal. He knew that what she saw was not promising. His rumpled peasant's tunic hadn't been washed in some time. His trousers were wrinkled and his shoes worn. But the red sash tied around his waist seemed to amuse her. Perhaps it reminded her of the nearly consumed fruit in her hand.

"*Oui*," she said, nodding curtly. "I will pose for you."

"Magnifique! Shall we begin?"

"I don't even know your name, nor you mine!" She pivoted as if to leave him.

"Wait," he said. "I am Monsieur Cézanne. Paul Cézanne."

She paused and glanced back over her shoulder. "I have not heard of you, Mr. Cézanne."

"Oh, but you will," he said.

She took the last bite of the apple and threw the core to a cheeky squirrel waiting beneath a potted tree. She swallowed slowly as she turned to face him.

"We shall see," she said, her lips pursed in a fetching pout. She fished a patterned handkerchief out of her breast pocket to blot her downturned mouth before extending her hand. "Mademoiselle Fiquet. Hortense Fiquet."

Young Woman With Her Hair Down, 1872

"So, you've captured him now," said Émile, staring at the small child suckling at the model's blue-veined breast. What did Paul see in this harridan?

"He has chosen me," said Hortense.

"He has chosen the placid oval of your face. Frankly, I'm not sure what he sees in the rest of you."

Émile turned towards the window of the cramped, grimy apartment and fingered the small green apple a veiled beggar woman had pressed on him as he entered the building. Thank goodness he no longer lived in reduced circumstances such as these. *Alleluia*, his novels provided much superior lodgings. How ironic, given where they'd started out, that he had become Paul's benefactor.

"Paul thinks you're his friend, but I see the cruelty beneath the kindness," said Hortense, moving the child to her other breast. "You consider this a contest of loyalty, but do not underestimate me. I will be loyal to him. I cannot say the same for you."

"How dare you question my fidelity to my oldest friend? I'm the one who supported him financially and emotionally ever since he moved to Paris. Even now, who is it that makes certain you and the boy are fed?"

"Who has been allowed to touch him?" hissed Hortense.

Émile winced at the mention of Paul's aversion to human contact.

The baby cried and Hortense stood to sooth him as she swayed back and forth. Émile retreated to the doorway but not before leaving the length of fine blue fabric on the shabby dresser top. He saw Hortense's eyes fix on the ornate ebony patterning.

"It is for him, for his paintings." He wanted her to know this gift was not something to work into her outlandish fashions.

She avoided his eyes and stared in silence at her now sleeping child.

Had she not been holding the baby he would have shaken her. Instead, he scolded her.

"Remember that he continues to be rejected by the Salon and by society. I am the one who champions him, who believes his genius will be recognized someday."

"And I am the one he captures with his genius." She lifted her head and cast a knowing glance at a half-finished canvas on the wall. There she was, her shoulders and breasts bared, framed by her long dark hair, her figure outlined in a verdant green, like the leaves of an apple tree in bloom.

"Bargh." Émile tripped down the stairs, anxious to be free of the small space that smelled of soiled baby linens. Once outside, he threw the apple at a small black dog with a crooked tail.

A Modern Olympia, 1873

Manet's *Olympia* had haunted Paul's dreams for ten years. The exquisite nude at the center of the painting appeared nightly to stare unabashedly at him, her invisible admirer, as he tossed and turned beside Hortense. Creating voyeurs out of every admirer had been Manet's triumph, earning him eventual acceptance by the Salon and everlasting notoriety as the leader of the avant-garde. If such images were what the gatekeepers wanted and the public would respond to, then Paul was determined to steal the erotic visions that ruined his sleep and paint a scene that would shock the art world into acknowledging him as well.

Both Hortense and the boy were sound asleep when he crept to his easel to take advantage of the light streaming from a high window. With a bit of charcoal, he outlined a small dog in the center of the painting, its crooked tail alert and apparently wagging—a symbol of the admirer's lust for the naked woman unveiled before him. Unlike the voyeur, the dog would face the viewer, openly panting with excitement.

Oh, how Paul understood the yearning to cast one's eye on naked flesh. The desire to merge beyond conventional barriers. Forget subtleties. This furry black surrogate would make obvious the voyeur's illicit connection at the precise moment his *objet de desir* was revealed.

Near the courtesan, he would place the original object of desire. An apple. No, many apples. In various degrees of ripeness, for man's desire was ever changing—one moment a flirtation, the next an obsession.

He sketched the golden fruit sitting even now on a nearby

table. Hortense had gathered it over the course of the last week. Offerings from an old beggar woman in the street. "Castoffs she'd likely stolen herself," Hortense said of the slowly-rotting orbs.

Still Life with Fruit Dish, 1880

I might as well have been a juggler, thought Paul, as he balanced the slippery fruit in shades of red, green, and orange on the white *compotier*. For weeks he'd tried to make more of these spheres than the masters who had come before him. Rather than the pleasing but static still life paintings of his mentor Pissarro, he intended to make others see the life in these orbs.

He'd listened to them whisper their interminable secrets, seen them preen for their portraits, heard them apologize for their changing colors. All to cause them to appear as though any moment they would roll out of the image and into the viewer's lap. The viewer and the viewed would know—nay, become—the other.

After a feverish few hours, he stood back and observed his work—was it genius or madness? He was too close to tell. He needed to see the work through another person's eyes. Specifically, through Hortense's inscrutable almond eyes. But she was gone for the day with the boy—whether to the gardens or the gambling hall, who could say?

Desperate for an opinion, he ran down the stairs and out into the streets. Near the small fountain at the corner an old woman sat knitting, her hands entangled in yarn the same drab color as her dark cloak. What would she know about color? But she was all he had.

He dashed towards her and thrust the painting in front of her.

"Tell me what you see," he demanded.

The woman lifted her veil. She scrutinized the painting as though she were one of the Salon members eager to once again reject his work. In the light of day, he realized his folly. He pulled back, ashamed to have submitted his vision to yet another critic.

The woman's grimace slowly spread into a welcome smile. She beamed at him, as though she were a proud parent. "It's astonishing, as I knew it would be."

Self Portrait and Apple, 1882

Paul returned from a troubled walk, eager to sketch a self-portrait. Grabbing his pencils and a scrap of paper, he balanced a chipped palette on his lap and studied his face in a small, clouded mirror. How fascinating the aging process. One day you are a boy swimming naked and laughing with your friends in the Arc, rescuing Émile from the current as you brush your waggish curls out of your eyes to discuss philosophy and pretty girls. And the next your pate is as round and smooth as an apple, while your hair has migrated from your skull to your chin.

He quickly sketched his own balding head and to the side added the apple Paul *fils* had left uneaten from their morning breakfast. Two spheres. Three really. Himself, his son, and the fruit. Where did one begin and one end? All were part of God's majesty and miracle.

His attempts to capture the divine essences—the motifs—of people and places had regularly been rejected. And yet his quest continued. "The world does not understand me, and I don't understand the world," he muttered as he added some cross-hatching to the right side of the apple–a bit of a beard to match his own.

He wasn't so certain about the Catholic rituals his mother and sister practiced back home, yet he believed God had given him these eyes, this brain, and these hands to share the souls of even the humblest of objects with the world. So, if his depictions of the grand peak of Mont Sainte-Victoire or the lush canyons of the human body would continue to be rejected, perhaps he should embrace the simplest of things. The fruit growing on the hillsides of his dear Aix had taught him everything he needed to know about life. This was the lesson he would share with the world.

The Basket of Apples, 1893

Even in old age, having returned to Aix, he wrestled with perspective. It was impossible to draw straight lines or fix end points. The only things that came easily were concentric circles that occasionally intersected like the apples before him in the basket, eager to spill into one's life like boules cast towards a jack.

He knew that's what his so-called friends called Hortense—a *boule*, a ball for sport. They found her common, couldn't see what she'd given him. Sometimes he denied her gifts as well, but he inevitably returned to her bed and to his portraits of her. He kept trying to capture the uncapturable.

He thought if he married her at last, that would help. Especially if he did so in front of his mother and his father. But even that didn't completely set things right. He couldn't align his life and his relationships with a brush stroke.

Same with Émile. The friend he'd once rescued, someone he thought he could depend on forever, had written that hateful book about him, called him a failure, depicted him as weak enough to commit the ultimate sin. Someone who would abandon the world, this rainbow of chaos, by his own hand. Something Paul would never do. Such betrayal astonished him. Curses on the little phrasemonger!

He grasped his knives and brushes. How fine and yet so

terrible to stand in front of a blank canvas. *Just begin*, he told himself as he drew circle after circle. Once again, these glorious orbs would speak for him.

Strange how the fruit had been left on his doorstep that morning. He'd seen a dark shadow disappear around a corner, just after the door knocker fell but before the basket was retrieved—so like the one Émile had presented him when they were just boys. There was no indication who had provided the gift. He shook his head to dispel the mystery. The work waited.

Everything in the painting would be as out of kilter as his relationships. The table would veer, the bottle would lean, the cookies would teeter, and the basket would tilt so that it could no longer contain the forbidden fruit. And the apples? The apples would roll forth into a world as unreliable as friendship, as inexplicable as love.

Author's Note

After years of rejection by the Paris Salon, the painter Paul Cézanne (1839-1906) turned from painting landscapes and nudes to vivid depictions of the humble fruit that had grown on the hillsides of his childhood village, Aix-en-Provence. At the time he famously declared "With an apple, I will astonish Paris."

His apples not only astonished Paris, but the world. Though his success came late in life, his career strongly influenced his Impressionist contemporaries and the Post-Impressionist artists who followed them. Many collected his paintings including Degas, Gauguin, and Monet. Both Pablo Picasso and Matisse called him "the father of us all."

A notable gift in his childhood was a basket of apples from a schoolmate—Émile Zola. Zola and Cézanne became fast friends until the publication of Zola's novel *The Masterpiece* which told the story of a failed artist thinly modeled after Cézanne. The novelist's unflattering depiction of his boyhood friend ruptured their friendship.

Cézanne's wife Hortense remains a mystery to the art world. Widely criticized by friends and family, Hortense nevertheless bore his only child and was the subject of at least twenty-nine portraits—a significant portion of his oeuvre.

THE LADY RANGER OF YOSEMITE

BY EDIE CAY

January, 1918

C lare watched the two old rangers in the chairs next to the river-stone fireplace out of the corner of her eye. Come high season, they wouldn't be allowed to take up space in the Sentinel Hotel's guest areas, but in a wartime January, there were no visitors. Archie Leonard inched his yellowed, gnarled hand closer to the fire. He already had a blanket on his lap, but it was clear he needed another. Anyone could tell Mr. Leonard's hands hurt, but no one would dare mention it, and certainly not Clare.

Perched on the great rim of Yosemite Valley, the hotel's windows and summer patio overlooked the spectacular formations of Clare's beloved park, now clad in a comfortable foot of snow. Even in the early winter darkness, the moon reflected the ghostly granite bubble of Half Dome across the gorge. She always thought of the feature like some great bald ogre, head cradled in his arms, snoring on the table that was the valley floor. As if she were ever in trouble, the massif would lift its head to defend her.

Clare turned the last chair upside down on the dining table, readying the Mountain House—the annexed dining room of the Sentinel Hotel—for her broom. During the low season, the Mountain House served as the Yosemite National Park staff headquarters. It was one of the reasons that Clare loved the low season. Fewer people meant that most of her hikes and rides were spent in serene solitude.

Some might raise an eyebrow at a young woman alone in the wilderness, but Yosemite had always felt safe to her, instantly like home, even on the first trip here with her parents when she was only thirteen. They had come in on horseback, uninformed and unprepared. Her parents had underestimated the time it would take to cross parts of the High Country, and the Army cavalry hunted them down at their ad hoc campsite when they didn't arrive at their proposed destination. Back then, the U.S. Army base at the Presidio in San Francisco staffed the park. It was different now with forest rangers and toll gates, and Clare wondered if life moved this fast for everyone. In the decade and a half since her first arrival in Yosemite, the whole world had changed: motorcars, telephones, war. As if with each passing year the vast globe shrank, meaner with every tick of the clock.

She went back into the kitchen to wring out the dishrag and found the enamel coffeepot a quarter full on the stove. If there was one thing her mother had instilled in her, it was to not waste a drop. Coffee made her feel like she had the shakes, so she took the pot out to the old rangers. Both men were hard of hearing, so they continued talking even as she approached.

"I can't make another season, Jack. It's my back, it's my hands, it's everything." Mr. Leonard tucked his gnarled knuckles under the blanket. His joints were bulbous and thick, the skin on his hands spotted and wrinkled like a sequoia's bark.

"Archie," Jack Gayler grumbled, shaking his head. "We're already down in numbers. Who is going to take in the gate receipts, let alone fight the fires?"

Mr. Leonard huffed out a gravelly chuckle. "I haven't been able to fight a fire in ten years and you know it. Look at me, Jack. Really look. You know something ain't right."

Mr. Gayler looked away, startling as Clare approached with the coffee. They were the oldest rangers, in their seventies, but stayed on because Yosemite was their home. Just like it was hers. Mr. Townsley, the rangers' supervisor, would never fire the men, and neither would quit. Mr. Gayler and Mr. Leonard were locked in a stand-off between time and duty, and no one wanted to interfere.

Clare respected both of them as her elders, of course, but she also found them worthy of admiration. They were romantic heroes of a sort, of a bygone and brutal past. In some ways, Clare wanted to be like them. She wanted to have that steel spine and unwavering sense of duty. But as the park's schoolmistress, she was unlikely to get the same respect for her dedication.

"Miss Hodges," Mr. Gayler greeted with a smile. He was missing a tooth on the side of his mouth, which made his grin appear lopsided. Clare liked that about him. It made him seem softer, less like a man haunted by the sins he'd committed in his younger years.

Both men came to Yosemite after serving in the Civil War, which seemed like ancient history to Clare. When they thought no one could hear them, they'd curse a streak so blue Clare thought God might smite them down that very instant. They always apologized if they thought she'd overheard. Both were always overly solicitous and danced with her at the employee functions, even though none of the young men ever did.

She knew they did it out of pity, but that was fine. Clare had other things she loved more than dancing. Sometimes Mr. Gayler said the mannerly things like, *if I were thirty years younger, I'd marry you in a heartbeat, Miss Hodges.*

But that was because she was polite, had a nice reading voice, and didn't mind refilling coffee cups and emptying ashtrays. Her handwriting was also excellent, though that was not generally a concern for men who might want to woo a twenty-seven-year-old spinster. Her birthday had been last month. She'd told no one.

Besides, she knew Mr. Gayler was doing his best to seem courtly, like Mr. Leonard was; still dancing with her, including her in conversations, and asking his wife Susie to take Clare under her wing, given Clare had taught several of their fifteen children. When Clare visited them at their home in the park, Susie and her extended family taught Clare how to identify Yosemite's plants and cures.

Susie was an Awani woman who'd been one of the last few of that tribe to be born in the valley, as her parents and grandparents and great-grandparents had before her. Most of the local tribes in the area had been forcefully dispersed by land management or quarrelling miners, while the women intermarried with white men. Still, Clare yearned to have that kind of tie to the land that Susie had, the undisputed identity to belong. Though, Susie would be the first to tell Clare that it didn't matter if one belonged to the land when there were Washington men—what she called the government—to take it away.

"More coffee?" Clare offered the rangers as she approached.

"You need to put some weight on, girl. Sneaking up on a couple of old men like that," Mr. Leonard complained.

"Ain't right to comment on a lady's figure, Archie. Hush up. Yes, Miss Hodges, we would both love some." Mr. Gayler leaned forward, showing off that empty hole in his smile.

Now that Clare was nearer, she could see how the bark-like skin on the backs of Mr. Leonard's hands were even more orange than before, and the whites of his eyes were almost the color of egg yolks. The schoolchildren had commented on it back in autumn, when he came to the classroom to help teach a lesson on animal tracks.

Mr. Leonard claimed that it was because when he was up in the High Country, he only ate carrots so his horse wouldn't feel left out. The children had laughed, and he'd given her a wink, pleased with his joke. But no amount of carrots turned a person that color.

In the winter, she didn't open the schoolroom when it got so cold. The children stayed home, helping their parents who lived and worked in the park. They were concessionaires, rangers, park supervisors, and hoteliers, married couples who wanted life somewhere different. Which also meant gathering plenty of firewood and food supplies for harsh days when snow kept the mountain passes impassable. During those weeks when the children stayed home, Clare helped out at the Mountain House.

Mr. Gayler let out an appreciative *ah* as she topped up his cup, and Mr. Leonard was already reaching into his inner coat pocket for his flask. She poured, leaving enough room for him to add his whiskey.

"What do you think spring will be like this year?" She asked, making conversation so she could enjoy the warmth of the fire, too. She hadn't realized how cold she was until she stopped working. Her toes and fingers burned as the heat seeped back in.

"Snow ain't too bad. Regular spring. As for the visitors?" Mr. Gayler let out a grunt and shook his head. He shuffled his feet, dirt from the treads falling in perfect straight lines.

Without thinking, Clare went to the woven basket by the side of the fireplace and retrieved two blankets. She put one over Mr. Leonard's already blanketed lap first, and then Mr. Gayler's. Her parents were older, so she knew about the cold that crept into bones and wouldn't let go.

"You are a treasure, Miss Hodges. Lucky be the man that

snaps you up." Mr. Leonard closed his eyes, propping his elbows on the chair's armrests, his gnarled hands resting on his stomach.

"Still going to be down a few rangers, I think," Mr. Gayler continued. "Wars always take too long. I don't know when our boys will be back."

"If they come back," Mr. Leonard griped.

"Our boys know land, even if it is in France. They know how to survive. And when they come back, we'll have their jobs waiting for them. I just don't know who can fill in 'til that day comes."

Despite how absurd it would sound, Clare wanted to yelp, *me! I could do it!* After two years of being the schoolmistress, fill-in maid, housekeeper, laundress, and Susie's acolyte, she knew all the buildings, trails, mountains, animals and plants. She had to teach all of it to the children. She knew how to treat poison oak, snake bites, and sprained ankles. She could make a fire without starting a wild one, and she preferred to go out on horseback alone. In fact, she'd spent most of last summer doing exactly that, since tourists had not flooded in as they had in years past.

"You'd make a good ranger, Miss Hodges," Mr. Leonard said.

Clare's heart leapt. She was greedy for compliments, and this was the finest she could ever receive.

"You're better on a horse than most of those greenhorns we get from the East," Mr. Leonard continued. "And you know the land."

Oh, she knew the land. And she loved the land. There was no better place in the world than Yosemite, with its waterfalls and iconic granite. There were sunny, warm summers, and snowy, soft winters. The smell was always sweet and pungent and perfect, filled with pine and manzanita. And it was home.

"Who ever heard of a lady ranger?" Clare teased back,

hoping to hide the want in her voice. The urge. Even though she'd be replaying his comment in her mind every night. *You'd make a good ranger, Miss Hodges.*

"Maybe you'd be the first," Mr. Gayler said, eyeing her with his watery blues. Mr. Leonard gave a thoughtful grunt that sounded like it could be approval.

It took Clare a month to work up the nerve to approach Mr. Townsley, the rangers' supervisor. The snow melted, and the Valley flooded as it typically did for a few weeks before it subsided and the ground absorbed the water it would need to last until the autumn rains. The fresh smell of pinesap and growing, verdant ferns filled the air. Brewer's blackbirds chirped their bright, squeaky calls on sunlit branches and in their rhythm she heard, *you'd make a good ranger, Miss Hodges.*

Despite the beautiful bright bluebird morning, with mountain-crisp air and warm sun on her skin, she crept towards the ranger headquarters as if it were midnight. As if she was afraid of disturbing the slumber of the taxidermied bear that stood guard just inside the front door of the ranger headquarters.

But within the last month, Mr. Leonard and Susie had left Yosemite for good—not moving far, but to a nearby town where he could see a doctor on the regular. His shakily scrawled letter said that the doc told him his liver and kidneys were bad. Mr. Gayler went to visit and when he returned, just shook his head and said that the Valley had kept Mr. Leonard alive, and leaving it had destroyed him.

Clare sometimes thought it would be the same for her. That leaving the park would be the worst thing that could ever happen. But if she were a ranger during the summer months when the schoolhouse was closed, then she would never have to leave. There weren't enough tourists to keep her picking up shifts at the Sentinel, not in any department. Newspapers reported American women going to Europe if they could speak French or German.

Clare knew French, technically, but it was schoolroom French mixed with French poetry, and her pronunciation was terrible. Certainly not of service to the war effort. Certainly not enough for her to leave Yosemite. There had to be other girls out there willing to leave their homes. And if Clare could be a ranger, then she would be doing her part, taking a job at home to support the men, so when they returned, their jobs would still exist.

At least, she told herself that she could be a placeholder for a man if that would keep the park open. If she had to help the war by staying indoors every day, her very soul would dry up and wither.

Inside the ranger headquarters, Clare gave a polite smile to the black bear that stood tall on its back legs, serving as both secretary and erstwhile hat stand, then knocked on Mr. Townsley's door. All of the buildings in the park smelled pleasantly of fresh cut lumber, even if they'd been there for years.

"Come in," came his cheerful voice. He was a good man and an excellent leader. His pleasant and polite demeanor was never ruffled, even when the Valley faced wildfires or floods, or worse —difficult tourists.

"Mr. Townsley," greeted Clare as she walked in. A wall of acrid funk hit her with the force of that black bear's paw. Immediately her eyes stung and watered, causing her vision to blur. Her head swam and she staggered.

"Oh, Miss Hodges, I do apologize," he said, his tools dropping to the desk with a clang. He hurried around his desk, dodging the taxidermied animals that decorated the room. Some of the creatures were small, like the adorable chipmunks with thin striped tails, and then some were large and imposing, like the bobcat whose tail permanently swished to the side so as to be on better display. Mr. Townsley's desk was littered with furry bits and strips of leather, an animal yet to be created.

She swayed, her vision swimming.

He cupped her elbow, hastening her out the door, past the black bear and down the front steps. "It's the glue. A very unpleasant scent if you aren't used to it."

She gasped and the nausea ebbed. She blinked away the tears over and over, the sensitive organs taking longer to recover. After a few deep breaths she no longer thought she would be seeing her breakfast a second time.

"That's why I keep the door closed and the windows open," he explained.

She nodded, still catching her breath, hoping she had not already failed in her quest. "That's quite an odor."

When she straightened, masking her remaining discomfort, he brightened. "What can I help you with, Miss Hodges?"

She adjusted her spectacles and her straw bonnet. "Well, I have, er—" She stumbled over her words. How did one ask for a job to the supervisor's face? Especially when he was such a nice man and wouldn't want to hurt her feelings when he inevitably turned her down? He probably had far more important things to do than speak with her.

His eyebrows remained raised, waiting for her to make her request.

Her father had once said she was a girl without fear—she could peer over Glacier Point, which hardly anyone could do without being gripped with terror. She spurred her horses to a full gallop regularly, with no concern of being flung off. She regularly camped overnight in the High Country alone, for Pete's sake. All she had to do right now was open her mouth.

If she never took a chance to ask for what she wanted, she'd kick herself for all the rest of her days. She took a breath to clear away all the hemming and hawing. This would have been better as a letter, but she would look foolish if she ran off without speaking. She had to fight for her chance to serve the park.

"Mr. Townsley." She pulled her shoulders back, and her heart threatened to leap from its post squarely in her chest. "Probably you'll laugh at me, but I want to be a ranger."

A grin spread across the man's face, and Clare waited for him to let out an unruly guffaw. But he didn't. The kindness for which he was known reached his eyes. "I beat you to it, young lady. It's been on my mind for some time to put a woman on one of these patrols, only I couldn't find the right one before."

Clare's eyes filled with glassy tears, but she blinked them back. "Truly?"

Townsley nodded. "I know how much you love this Valley—"

"—Not just the Valley," Clare interrupted, wanting to be clear that she wouldn't play favorites with her territory, just like she didn't play favorites with her students. "But the High Country, too."

Townsley nodded, his expression clear that he was waiting for her to finish.

"I mean, I will go wherever assigned, of course. Wherever is needed."

"Well, we're short on rangers, regardless. Especially with Art going off to the Army."

Clare nodded, hoping that she was not somehow endangering her mortal soul for hoping Arthur Gallison liked being in the Army so much that he didn't return. She certainly didn't want to wish him dead. Just happiness elsewhere. So she could keep his job.

"I'll have to check with the higher-ups. You'd be the first

woman park ranger, as far as I know, so we have to clear it with the National Park Service. And this is the seasonal position, to be clear. Not Art's permanent position."

Clare probably looked like a silly girl, standing there, wobbling, trying to look capable, when she felt anything but. Being unmarried and twenty-seven, there were few things that people thought her capable of, other than teaching children.

"I'm sure it'll take a few weeks, Miss Hodges, but in the meantime, why don't you talk with Jack about it. See where he thinks you fit in the roster. He knows this park as well as anybody."

She didn't want to say that she'd already spoken with him— that it was him and Mr. Leonard who had given her hope. *You'd make a good ranger, Miss Hodges.* Instead, she grabbed Mr. Townsley's calloused hand and shook it with both of hers. "Thank you so much for considering me, Mr. Townsley. You can't imagine how grateful I am."

He laughed and extracted himself, and only then did Clare realize that she was being too eager, too earnest. Her beloved Yosemite needed her, and she would always be there for the park.

July, 1918

The seasonal ranger position hadn't begun until June, which had fit well with ending the school year with the children. Clare had handed over the schoolhouse key to Mr. Townsley for safe-keeping until the next schoolmistress showed up, and her pocket felt so much lighter without that iron weight. Other women might be sad to lose the security of a teaching position, but

Clare could be a seasonal ranger as late as October, so she could not have both jobs. The gamble was worth it, in Clare's opinion.

Besides, today she was a ranger. They'd even taken a picture of all them on horseback for the 1918 season and *included her*. The permanent rangers were in the new uniforms, while the temporary rangers wore their usual working clothing. For Clare, she wore wide-legged gaucho trousers, which hid the shape of her leg, but made riding astride her roan gelding, Red, safe and comfortable.

It was strange to wear trousers every day—a far cry from the hygiene code for schoolmistresses. There were no edicts about her hair, her glasses, her undergarments. There were, however, prudent guidelines for footwear and hats. She wore the same wide-brimmed felt Stetson-style as the other rangers, as it kept out the sun and was heavy enough that the wind wouldn't blow it off, unlike her flimsy summer straw bonnets.

There had been a fair amount of curiosity from the other women in Yosemite, like Kitty Tatsch who worked sundries, and Mrs. Michael, who helped her husband run Camp Curry. Mrs. Michael seemed scandalized that trousers were part of Clare's uniform, even though Mrs. Michael spent most of her life outside.

The other rangers accepted her easily, thanks in no small part to Jack Gayler. Because of her new position, Mr. Gayler insisted she call him Jack, which was still unsettling. He was older than her father. Slowly, he doled out tasks that he thought she could handle, and as she excelled, so did his trust in her abilities.

Today's job was the most daring yet, though it was not anything she had not done on her own before. She was to pick up the gate receipts from the eastern entrance. Though simple in description, it meant carrying a bag of money through the wilderness and required an overnight journey. It took most of a day to get out to the eastern gate, and yet another to return. It was once Mr. Leonard's job, now passed on to her. She once again thought of his yellowed, gnarled hands and sent a simple prayer skyward. The news was that his health was improving, thanks to regular doctoring and Susie's watchful eye. Mr. Gayler —Jack—brought water from Yosemite's streams to him every month, just in case that was what kept him healthy.

As Clare checked Red's saddle, and finished stowing the saddlebags, Mr. Gayler approached, leading his donkey, Samson. "I'd be happy to ride with you, part ways at least," he said, a toothpick in the side of his mouth.

Clare knew that he was trying to protect her, make her feel comfortable, but the offer was like a burr in her sock. "No thank you, Mr. Gayler. I've ridden this trail a hundred times. I wouldn't want to take you from your tasks."

He grunted and examined Red's saddle, as if he were about to check her work. As if she'd never saddled a horse before. This was a test of wills, and she wasn't going to start her first real task on anyone else's terms.

"Where's yer weapon?"

"I have my field knife in my pack."

"I mean a rifle." Mr. Gayler looked pointedly at the bedroll on the back of the saddle, where many rangers stowed theirs.

She stopped her work with the saddle and turned to him, as she would any child that was pestering her. "I have no intention of carrying a rifle. You've seen me. I can't hit the broadside of a barn. Besides, it's extra weight for Red and me. It's a nuisance."

"Take mine," he said, pulling his Winchester out of the rifle holster he kept on Samson's saddle. "I'd offer my .45, but it'd be too heavy for you."

When she demurred, he pushed the carbine into her hands. She pushed it back into his arms, and not wanting to go into details said, "One only carries a gun if one intends to kill a creature. I have no intention of killing anything."

Jack narrowed his eyes at her and she could see the iron-spined soldier he'd once been. A man who had killed his fellow man. Someone who had seen the horrors of a battlefield. There was something deeper than steel in his gaze—remorse or guilt or righteousness, she didn't know. She didn't want to know. His world had been full of grime and ash and fear, and it only reminded her of the war that lay beyond the boundaries of her beloved park.

The only thing that kept the smell of fear and grit away was not acknowledging it. With her poor eyesight and distracted demeanor, she had no chance against a charging bear or a marauding bandit. What was the point? She wasn't exchanging her peace for the illusion of protection.

"We know for a fact that there are poachers using park land. And there's always some old miner hiding, hoping for gold. You need to protect yourself." Jack rolled his breakfast toothpick over to the side of his mouth, which was now a firm line with a downward tick on one side. "You'll be carrying the gate receipts. Standard protocol is to carry a weapon."

"Mr. Gayl—"

"—Jack," he corrected her.

"Jack." She took a breath, hoping to buy herself a moment to compose her thoughts. "I have shot rifles before. I've even used a six-shooter. I'm both clumsy and a terrible shot."

"If you weren't scribbling in your little book every five minutes, you'd be more aware of your surroundings. See my scabbard on Samson?" He pointed to his saddled donkey. "It's a quick draw to get the Winchester out. Easiest thing."

"I don't have a scabbard," she said, gesturing to Red, who was ready and saddled, shifting his weight, waiting for her.

"You can use mine," Jack insisted.

Not knowing what else to do, she drew herself up as a schoolmistress and looked down her glasses at him. They were the same height, her in her riding boots, and him permanently hunched over like the letter C.

"I will not be taking a firearm into the High Country. I won't use it, and I don't want anyone using it on me."

Jack blinked as if she had slapped him across the cheek. The sun caught the gray and white bristles that studded his face. He screwed up his mouth as if he might protest, but then removed the toothpick and said, "Fine," with all the venom of a child who lost an argument.

Mr. Gayler returned his rifle to its scabbard and Clare swung her leg over Red's wide back. The saddle creaked as she adjusted her weight. "I'll be fine," she assured him, but he didn't stop glowering at her.

He mounted Samson, stowing the Winchester and settling in the saddle. "See that you are." He rode off before she could give him any more assurances.

Clare patted Red's neck, thanking him silently for being her reliable companion, and they headed off toward the eastern gate. The path took them to the far end of the Valley, then up the switchbacks that ate up daylight. Clare rested them in Tuolumne Meadows, reveling in the smell of sunshine warming the scattered pine needles across the forest floor, the redwood sweetness of the sequoias from the Mariposa grove, and the glacial freshness from the just-above-freezing Tenaya Lake. This was the most potent perfume in the world, and she wouldn't trade it for anything. This was Eden.

She saddled up again, wanting to reach her destination with ample time. Passing through the Grand Canyon of the Tuolumne, they found relief in the dappled shade and cooler temperature. Yet her conversation with Mr. Gayler disturbed her enjoyment of a perfect afternoon. Should she have brought a weapon?

She inhaled the perfect Yosemite scent that had inspired her poem "The Land of Wandering," which had been published in the *Pacific Short Story Club Magazine*, and caught the attention of several fellow Yosemite employees. Some even called her their own Yosemite poetess.

Recalling her poetry, the question of a weapon was forgotten. She dug through her trouser pockets, big and loose in her gaucho pant legs. Fishing out her pencil and notebook, she started jotting down a new poem, imagining the words fluttering down upon her like butterflies and autumn leaves.

> *Thy shimmering robe of meadow green,*
> *Thy sparkling dew on blade and tree*
> *Thy jeweled veil, Tuolumne...*

The wilderness was limitless in beauty. And here, the beauty included her, in the way that beauty in the "civilized" world did not.

September, 1918

Clare knew before Mr. Townsley said it. The rangers all knew it. The hotel staff and the concessionaires all knew.

Arthur Gallison had come home. While his unit reorganized, Arthur was not going back. She had known she would be among the first rangers laid off. Mr. Townsley had said *temporary*, but she had hoped for more than a mere two months.

She was of course grateful that Arthur Gallison came home with both arms and both legs, ready to return to patrolling the High Country, putting out wildfires, and scaring off the grazing trespassers. It didn't help that she lived in a bunkhouse with the new schoolteacher, the one who had been hired to take her position while she took Mr. Gallison's.

She waited until the woman snored softly so that she could weep into her pillow. There were no other positions for her to take. How would she feed herself? How would she stay in the Valley, now that Art had returned? It had been a gamble, but she hadn't thought she'd lose so quickly.

The world was still at war. Newspapers talked of Spanish influenza sweeping California. That there had been cases where a person woke up with a runny nose and died by dinner. But here in Yosemite, the birds still chirped and the chipmunks still patrolled the garbage cans.

How was she supposed to go back into a city when that was the world she would enter? But she didn't have a choice. Her professor at the San Jose Normal School, where she'd graduated, had once told her that they'd always find a position for her. Her only option for a living wage had been to send off letters, begging for a placement.

Her breath made the pocket under the woolen blanket humid. She was twenty-seven and alone. If she'd had any looks to trade on, or any reasonable domestic instinct, she would have already married long ago. As it was, she was only magazine-famous, at least in the ladies' journals circulation. She'd given interviews via letters, had her picture taken, and sent off a few more poems, which were accepted largely because of her status as the Lady Ranger.

She was not the only one, as there was another lady ranger at Mount Rainier, but Clare had been hired first. The journalists seemed to like that—her being "the first." More than one had offered her a roll in the hay, to which she smiled firmly and politely, recalled her schoolmistress voice and declined. Besides, they only wanted to bed her because they thought she was daring. But that was Kitty Tasch, not her. Kitty was the one who'd danced on Glacier Point for a photographer and still happily autographed any pictures that circulated near her.

But being a ranger was more impressive than a high-kick, and Clare could admit it had romantic appeal. She'd loved her work this past summer more than anything. And she'd felt that respect that she'd craved—the kind the world gave to the Jack Gaylers and Archie Leonards of the world.

Her chest hurt when she thought about leaving. She turned the idea in her head for days, letting Red's easy gait soothe her wounded heart as they took their last patrols. She'd miss Red, of course. And all the rangers, the children, the other women. Even though they were useless, she'd miss all of those college-boy blowhards who took up summer work, too. But part of being self-sufficient, as she liked to believe herself to be, was making difficult choices.

At least she had drafted dozens of poems in her notebook. They were works that she could tend to over the winter when she longed to feel that hot sun on her skin while a gentle pine breeze kept her cool.

And so, on her last day of work, she brushed Red far longer than was needed. She put her hand on every splintering wooden building, every rough-barked oak and pine. She touched the wide expanses of the boulders and dipped her hand in the streams at the bottom of the seasonally-trickling waterfalls.

The granite dome did not lift his head to say goodbye. She had to carry that as an omen. All she had to do was figure out how to return.

The San Jose Normal School did not technically qualify as hustle-bustle. But to Clare it felt like it. She had arrived too late to receive a teaching position, as she should have known, and the campus was in an upset because the much-beloved chancellor had died of Spanish influenza. Clare was frugal, and rented a room in a boarding house for women close to the campus.

She could have returned to her parents—well, her mother and her mother's new husband. But she felt that she needed to prove herself. At twenty-seven, with twenty-eight rapidly approaching, she could manage on her own. Besides, how was she to get from Santa Cruz to San Jose for daily tutoring sessions?

The landlady, Mrs. Ward, told her that her weekly payments were for room and board, but the very next day had taken ill like so many others. Neither Clare nor the other boarders had wanted to go near her for fear of contamination, so her son came and retrieved her by wagon. Clare had watched from her window. Then she went to the pantry and snitched the last can of peaches, scared that this would be the last food she would receive in exchange for an entire week's worth of rent.

On the next Sunday afternoon, when rent was due, the boarding house received a visit from Mr. Ward, the landlady's son. He was somber, held his dusty bowler in his hand and apologized that there had been no food provided. He asked for a reduced rent, and then told the ladies to go to the Kelly Brothers grocery, where Mrs. Ward kept an account.

After Mr. Ward left, the three young ladies all looked at each other. This was the only time they'd been all in the same room. Clare was the oldest by far, but there was something about them that seemed similar. All of them were thin and bookish, which made sense, given the house's proximity to the school.

"Should we draw straws?" The one who also wore spectacles asked.

"Do you not like shopping?" Clare asked, genuinely curious. She didn't mind it. And given that she didn't have a real job and was sick of eating nothing but porridge in her room, she'd wanted to do the shopping.

The other two girls shook their heads emphatically. So Clare dared a smile and said, "I'll take care of it."

The Kelly Brothers grocer was a little more than a half mile from the house, and Clare loved any excuse for a walk. The streets were empty as the epidemic raged. Every house had been afflicted, or at least, that's what the *San Jose Mercury Herald* announced in its inky pages. Clare believed it, but she also believed that the touch of sunshine and a good walk cured most anything.

Kelly Brothers was a decent sized storefront, with canned goods stacked in the windows. A thin screen door banged gently in the breeze. She entered, covering her eyes as she adjusted to the dim light, and she heard the greeting from the man behind the counter. The voice sounded familiar, but when she rifled through her brain for who it might be, nothing fit. She dropped her hand, and her eyes met a friendly face.

"Miss Hodges!" the clerk exclaimed, recognizing her right away, even at a ten foot distance. Behind the counter was none other than Earle Seiverson. They'd met at the San Jose Normal School years ago, and she'd helped him with his English papers, and he'd helped her with math. She hadn't really needed the help, but he'd wanted to reciprocate, so she let him.

She tried to tame the grin that erupted on her face. "Mr. Seiverson. I had no idea you were still in town."

He nodded, then frowned as he glanced about the store, with its shelves of dry goods, and canned produce. There were boxes of fresh vegetables and fruit behind him. He had graduated with a degree in mechanical engineering, during the time she earned her teaching certificate.

"I work here, at the moment," he said, dropping his eyes from hers.

The front of the store was dusty from the street, but she ventured further in, drawn in not only by the abundance of food, but also by Earle Seiverson. He watched her with sparkling brown eyes, as if she were a star. His hair was slicked back with pomade, and his shoulders had filled out.

"Are you still Miss Hodges? I saw your picture in a magazine just last week, if you don't mind me saying so."

She inclined her head, suddenly proud of those interviews and photographs. "I am still Miss Hodges." *He wanted to know if she was married!* Her, Clare Hodges.

"You really were a park ranger?" He sounded awed by her, and she liked it. The magazine articles had made her feel funny, as if she were a fraud waiting to be found out. But when Earle Seiverson looked at her that way, she felt taller in her boots.

"I really was. Rode into the High Country alone. Checked campsites. I once helped a lady hiker who had sprained her ankle. Oh, and I helped a group of gentlemen who had accidentally camped in poison oak."

The look of pained and amused empathy on Earle Seiverson's face made her smile. "I bet they were grateful."

"They would have been more grateful if I'd showed up the night before to show them what poison oak looked like," she said, and that made him laugh. "Is your mother still the Train Depot matron?"

"'Til her dying breath," he said, but his eyes were so focused on her, so profound, that it didn't seem like he understood that she had changed the subject from herself to his family.

She didn't buy enough supplies for the whole week at the boarding house. Instead, she returned the next day and then the next, inventing excuses to see Earle Seiverson as often as possible.

And when he asked if she'd like to come to dinner at his mother's house, her heart leapt.

Twenty-seven years old, and she had a suitor.

October, 1918

A whirlwind romance, one of Earle's sister-in-laws, Arlie Seiverson, wrote to her, congratulating them on their sudden nuptials. It had been a busy six weeks. Not many understood that despite not quite two months from being reintroduced, Clare had known Earle for years. She knew that he was from a good family: his mother was dubbed the "Mother of the Depot" by the newspaper, for her daily volunteer work of greeting travelers on the train system, especially the young women and children, helping them get safely to their families and boarding houses.

And his youngest sister, Miss Josephine, was also a pillar in the community. She had a quilting society that moved from house to house every week to entertain shut-ins and wounded soldiers. Now that influenza had scorched its way through the area, Miss Josephine cared for the sick as much as she was able. As the temperatures cooled, the virus seemed to be spreading again, and while there was concern for Josephine, there was faith that God would keep her safe.

Now married without fanfare, with at least her mother in attendance, they moved to a small rental house in Santa Clara where Clare would stay while Earle joined the U.S. Army. The epidemic had affected troop deployments, and while Clare was happy to be married, she couldn't help but wish this had happened before Art Gallison had been sent home.

A new influx of men was required as the war continued, and Earle's mechanical engineering degree could be put to good use fixing machines rather than fighting. After all, the plant he had worked at had shut down when the government diverted all materials to the war effort. By enlisting, Earle could do his part now, which Clare supported so much that she bought a fifty-dollar bond out of patriotism. When her name was printed in the paper, it led to their first fight—she'd spent money without his knowledge.

Now living in a new area, Clare hoped to pick up a teaching position. Once again, she waited on the misfortune of a man going to war to make an opportunity. She knew she was clever. It was sometimes dispiriting to have conversations with Earle, because it became evident that she was smarter and more worldly than her husband. She tried very hard to consider that they were smart in different areas, but when she helped him brush up on his engineering knowledge for his Army placement test, she grew frustrated with his slower recall.

There, in their little rented house, cozied up at the small wooden table, Clare realized that she now had to pretend to not comprehend here just as she had to in school. That living with this man meant she'd have to push aside her true self. The night of that realization, Earle rolled over to her and ran his hand along her hip. They were newlyweds, after all. It was a fumbling experience, but getting more enjoyable every time. As she rolled toward him, wanting the intimacy, she realized that this too, was subsuming herself. That despite what she wanted, this aspect of her life was one she no longer controlled either.

As the days passed, Earle fretted over his looming departure. Scheduled to leave the third week of November, it was a shock when mere days before Earle's deployment, the radios and newspapers erupted with the joyous news that the war was over. Earle would stay home.

November, 1918

The news of victory put people in the streets for celebration. But the virus did not care. Two weeks after the announcement, Earle's sister Josephine died from Spanish influenza. She could not have a public funeral, and the family was told to stay away from the burial site. God had not saved her. Josephine had not been chosen for a holy calling—she was as human as the rest of them.

Clare bit her lip, not knowing what to say as Mrs. Seiverson and Earle wept, clinging to one another. Josephine was the daughter who stayed home, a virtuous companion to Mrs. Seiverson's duty-bound life and Earle's bachelor existence. Clare's stomach churned as she made sandwiches when the other grown Seiverson children arrived at her mother-in-law's house. Clare made tea and coffee for the family, dusted off a recipe for coffee cake that was bookmarked in one of Mrs. Seiverson's well-worn cookbooks.

It was odd that even though Clare normally loved sweets, mixing the batter with a large wooden spoon was the hardest thing she'd ever done. Every few seconds, she ran to the back door, flinging it open to breathe some fresh air, her stomach threatening to empty its contents.

Arlie, one of her new sisters-in-law, walked into the kitchen just as Clare made her mad dash. She took over the stirring as Clare explained her difficulty. Arlie's three children ran through the room, making a hasty exit to the backyard. Then came two older children and another sister-in-law arrived in the kitchen.

Arlie explained to Carrie, Earle's sister, about Clare's sensitivity, and a knowing look passed between them. Finally, as Arlie poured the batter into the floured baking pan, Carrie put her hand on Clare's arm. "Darling. You're pregnant."

February, 1919

Earle remained unmoored in the face of his sister's death. He was a bulky, brooding presence when he was home, unresponsive and smoking cigars constantly while he stared at nothing out the window. The normally devout family had not bothered with church, staying home excused by the flurry of influenza deaths. God had broken the trust of Earle Seiverson, and he was not going to forget it.

The smell of the smoke made Clare sick, and she made him bathe after each one, until he started to refuse. She then started sleeping on the couch, rather than wake up in the middle of the night to retch. She cleaned the bathroom with vinegar, polished the furniture with lemon juice, and opened the windows, shivering in her coat and scarf, trying to empty out the scent of stale cigars and unbearable depression.

How horrible was it that Clare had wished the war had gone just a little longer so that Earle would have deployed? She squeezed her eyes shut, her fingers numb with cold, and her toes frozen stiff. Once again, she wished for the worst only to benefit herself. She must be right up there with the devil. But she'd rather have an absent husband than this morose chimney.

She'd tried everything she could think of, most of them suggestions from her mother-in-law. Clare made meatloaves and cakes, borrowed gramophones and even a radio. She tried to take him out for walks on weekends, and even arranged a weekend motorcar trip with friends to Mariposa, hoping the fresh air would cheer them both.

It was as close as she'd been able to get to Yosemite in months. She missed the park every day, dreamed of it every night. The smell of the pines and warmth of the winter sun had made Clare glow. There she felt alive. There was the place for her baby. How strong that baby would be up in the mountains, where the ground thrummed with life. The birds called and chirped and flew about the branches, smears of bright blues and bright reds. The little black ones with a yellow breast. And in the summer, hummingbirds with shiny crimson heads and bright green bodies would dart this way and that.

She'd sat on the porch steps in Mariposa, her belly a round little hardness, so different from her normally fleshy abdomen. The sun had been perfectly welcoming, and all she could think about was how she would introduce her baby to Yosemite. A blanket in the open meadow of the Valley, letting the baby loll about, turning to gaze up at El Capitan, Half-Dome, Bridalveil Falls, and Glacier Point. And how those formations would adore her child right back.

"I can't wait to meet you," she'd whispered to her belly. This was the only thing that was all *hers*. And she didn't want to share it with Earle.

They had returned to their cold rented cottage in Santa Clara on Sunday. All Clare could think was that she didn't want to enter. She wanted to be anywhere but there.

September, 1919

Having a baby was not as easy as it looked. Her few memories of the event centered around the feeling of being ripped in half like a piece of paper. Because of Mrs. Seiverson, Clare had gone to the hospital during her labor, even though she'd wanted to stay at home with her mother, who had a bathtub to help ease the pain.

In the hospital, Clare woke from a doze when a nurse crept in and asked Earle in a whisper what the baby's name was so they could fill out a birth certificate. All Earle could do was stare. Hurt clouded Clare's mind, but she kept her voice even. "We haven't decided quite yet. How long do we have?"

In the end, Earle said he *didn't care* what the baby's name was, so Clare ignored traditions of naming a boy-child after his father or grandfather and named the baby what she wanted: Forest Glen. It reminded her of Yosemite and sunshine and peace.

Though peace was not what Clare received. No one had told her that she would continue to bleed. Or that Forest would scream if she put him down for even a moment. She scrubbed the baby's rags, hung them up in the cooling afternoon sun. The battle of clean cloths versus no screaming occupied all of the space in her brain. She slept little, like all new mothers. Her feet hurt, the skin of her fingers and hands cracked from scrubbing, and still she bled.

One evening, Earle came home to find her sleeping on the cold kitchen floor, nested next to the stove, the baby diaperless, but covered with a blanket.

He shook her awake, a large, rough hand on her shoulder. "Where's dinner?"

She blinked at him, unable to comprehend what he was asking. Where was it? Another thing she needed to find. She sat up, careful not to disturb Forest, who stirred as the warm pocket next to him shifted. "What?" Her eyes felt like sandpaper. Her milk was engorged and it was time for another feeding. She'd have to wake Forest soon so that her breasts didn't clog again.

"You're supposed to cook dinner," Earle said.

Had he even said her name? She squinted, one eye open, the other blissfully closed. She was supposed to keep the baby alive, which kept her surprisingly busy. They hadn't the money to pay for a diaper service, and Earle refused to take advantage of his time at the grocery, saying Clare should be responsible for the shopping, since she was supposed to be the one making dinners. "I didn't cook. I think there is enough for sandwiches, if you can give me a moment."

Earle turned on his heel and put his jacket back on. Clare stood up, feeling blood leave her body in a flush of warmth between her legs. Dear God, when would that stop? She hurried over to the door. "Where are you going?"

"My mother's. She'll cook for me."

Clare nodded. Would Mrs. Seiverson take care of her, too? She needed help. She needed someone. "Could you bring something back?"

In the kitchen, Forest began to cry. Clare's milk let down, and the front of her shirt dampened. Earle noticed, staring at her chest as if he couldn't figure out where the liquid had come from. Then he left.

There was something that severed irrevocably as she watched him go. The idea that Earle had once trumpeted about help-meets broke into shards, like a glass breaking on concrete. He'd said they were a team, facing this world together. But she realized that only worked when they were both at their best. When she was the Lady Ranger, and he was a mechanical engineer—which had been before the war. But when she was a new mother and he was a clerk at a mercantile, what were they?

At least once the baby was born, Clare and Forest took the bed and Earle slept on the couch. Alone again, Clare buttered a slice of bread and took it with her up to bed with Forest. She nursed him while she ate and then they both fell into another slumbering pile.

This time Clare dreamed. She hadn't dreamt in weeks—unable to clear out the tumbling stress of her every day existence. But in this dream, she and Forest were in the Valley, in the meadow, the smell of pine and sweetness in her nose, the sun on her arms and face. She looked down at her baby, kicking and burbling on his blanket. There was a loud noise, but it didn't startle either of them. She looked up to find Half-Dome had risen his head, a giant bald-pated father, and looked down with affection at the wriggling baby, who danced on his back in happiness.

In this dream, it felt that Half-Dome was Forest's father, not Earle, because it was the mountain who loved the child most after her. That knowledge made her heart full in a way that it had never been before. She looked up at Half-Dome, grateful for his love for her child, and in turn, Half-Dome met her eyes with fondness in a way Earle had never done.

When she woke up, the feeling lingered. Jack Gayler's words about Mr. Leonard rang in her mind, that it was Yosemite that had kept him alive all those years, and leaving the park would kill him. And then Mr. Leonard's words came back all at once: *you'd make a good ranger, Miss Hodges.*

1921

Clare was thirty years old and Forest was only three months when she left Earle. They moved in with her mother in Santa Cruz, and Clare got a teaching job in the autumn. It wasn't the same as returning to Yosemite, but the Big Basin Redwoods nearby gave her enough balance until the following summer, when she and Forest worked at a camp near Yosemite.

Jack Gayler was gone from the rangers—retired and living in Stockton. The young college boys looked the same as they ever had, even though it was a different rotation every year. Kitty Tasch remained, as did the Michaels, tending to Camp Curry. Occasionally, local ranchers showed up to those employee dances and brought her lemonade as she let Forest bob his knees to the fiddle music.

Forest was already toddling about when Clare finally laid out a blanket in the middle of the expansive Valley meadow. While Half-Dome never shifted and raised his head, she still felt affection from the protective granite walls that surrounded her, welcoming her and her baby home.

Author's Note

This is a true story. Clare Hodges was the first paid female park ranger in the National Park Service. She began as a schoolmistress in Yosemite, and because she was encouraged by the older rangers, wrote to Mr. Townsley, asking for a position. The verbal dialogue in my story is taken directly from their letters. Because this is a short story, I changed the details to a face-to-face discussion. Mr. Townsley was regarded by all as a very nice man, and very competent, who loved his taxidermy. The smell of his hobby, however, was not beloved by all.

All the rangers mentioned by name are real, as was Susie, the Awani woman who was born in Yosemite. Of the Me-wuk people, the group that lived in the village of Awani/Ahwahnee was designated by the name. Clare spelled the name Awani, which is why I used that spelling here. The Me-wuk were not recognized as a tribe until 1924, and were largely referred to as "Digger Indians" prior to that. Thus, Susie would have identified as belonging to the Awani group of people.

The real life Susie signed a letter of protest that was sent to Washington when the U.S. Army took over her homeland without recompense. There were many excuses given as to why the American government would take the land, but people had been living in and around the Yosemite Valley long before white people ever graced the shores of the west coast. Susie and some of her female relatives stayed on in the park, providing demonstrations of traditional domestic arts.

Clare's short-lived stint as a park ranger did make it easier for women to enter the park service in later decades, but it still took a long time to overcome the gender barrier. Clare returned to the San Jose Normal School after her time in Yosemite, where she met an old friend and schoolmate, Earle Seiverson. His mother's name graced the *San Jose Mercury Herald* several times for her dedication to meeting young women and children who stepped off the train in San Jose. Earle's sister Josephine was also community driven, and all her activities noted in this story are factual, including her death from influenza.

I don't know why Clare and Earle divorced, but I kept the

dates accurate. I also don't know why they married. Earle was trained as a mechanical engineer, he was set to enter the U.S. Army, and he was working as a clerk in a grocery store when they reacquainted themselves during their whirlwind romance. They even took that car trip to Mariposa, as was reported in the *San Jose Mercury News*. Forest Glen was indeed born that year as well.

I'm happy to say that Clare had a happy-ever-after, as much as one can find in real life. During her work at one of the myriad camps near the entrance to Yosemite, Clare met a cattle rancher from Mariposa by the name of Peter Wolfsen. He was older than her, but they both dedicated their lives to the area, and married in 1925. Forest Glen also lived a healthy life. With Wolfsen, Clare guided and helped out at Camp Wawona, which is near the entrance to Yosemite National Park.

The water in Yosemite is considered by some to have extra powers of longevity. I don't personally believe it, but some do. I think just being in the natural world is enough. However, that's why I added the detail of Jack bringing Archie the water—for its healing properties.

On a personal note, I live near Yosemite. This is the second story I've set in the park, and I have a feeling it won't be the last. If you haven't visited, you don't know the magic. I encourage you to find time to change that. You might find something you didn't know you were missing.

THE SPIES' DILEMMA
JONATHAN POSNER

Chapter One

Before dawn, the cellar of a Thameside tavern
April 21, 1536

The ropes cut into the young man's wrists, but he kept an upward pressure on the bonds. Better that than letting the sharp stones pushed beneath each wrist pierce up into his flesh. Trying to ignore the pain from the hours he had been bound this way to the arms of the chair, he shifted slightly in his seat. As if he could find a position with even a fraction more comfort. As if he were not being held captive in this pitch-black cellar.

There was a scrabbling noise and a low squeak, followed by the feel of claws gripping the toe of his boot, then the weight of what must have been a large rat.

"Begone, fellow," the man said aloud, twitching his foot. It was a slight movement, given how tight his ankle was also tied to the leg of the chair, but it was enough. There was a thump as the rat jumped down.

"Too bad you did not think to chew through the bonds, my friend," the man muttered as it scuttled away.

The door opened and the two Spaniards returned; their heavy glass lamps casting a dim glow around the small cellar.

"You said something, señor?" asked the taller one. It sounded like a pleasant inquiry, but the young man knew it was anything but. He kept silent. He had no inclination to talk.

The other Spaniard, the shorter and stockier one, held his lamp to the Englishman's face.

"No matter. I expect you have not slept since we left you here last evening. So now you will tell us what we need to know. And if lack of sleep has dulled your wits, belike this will sharpen them." He took a loop of fresh rope from his belt and slipped it over the man's left wrist. Then he produced a stick, about the length of his forearm, and pushed it through the loose rope below the chair's arm. The Spaniard gave it several turns, until it pulled his wrist down onto the stone.

The tall man came round and stood beside his fellow countryman. "He makes another full turn and it will sever your wrist. All your blood will leave your body. So tell us, señor spy, the answers to what we asked last evening."

He nodded at the other Spaniard, who turned the stick a fraction.

The young man gasped, straining against the rope. "I cannot tell what I do not know," he whispered.

"Por Dios! We have observed you coming from Secretary Cromwell's house more than once. You clearly work for him—and what he knows, you will also know. So tell us. The heretic concubine who styles herself 'Queen'—Anne Boleyn. Is she fallen from favor? Will she be cast away like the true Queen Katherine and sent to a nunnery?"

"I am not—" the young man began, then paused for the smallest moment. He had seen what the two Spaniards, with their backs to the door, had not. It had opened a fraction. A small dark figure had slipped in. "I am not privy to such information. You mistake me. I am but a hard-working lawyer."

The figure slid silently up behind the shorter Spaniard. "Even a lawyer—" the man began, but he got no further. There was a thump; he gave a gasp and his eyes widened. Slumping forward onto the bound man's knees, he slid to the floor. The burning lamp rolled to a stop beside the body.

A knife hilt stood proud from the stocky back.

"Por Dios!" the other Spaniard barked. There was a metallic swish as he drew his sword. He held up his own lamp and stared into each corner of the room. "Show yourself!"

The figure remained unseen.

"Very well!" The Spaniard put the tip of his blade against the young prisoner's chest. "You come to save this spy? Show yourself, or I run him through."

There was a soft laugh from his left. His head flicked round. A dark shadow flitted to his right. Suddenly the dead Spaniard's lamp rose up, as if it had gained the gift of flight. The man in the chair caught a momentary glimpse of a hooded figure, then the lamp swung at the tall man's head. It connected with a thump and the Spaniard staggered back, dropping his sword and falling. The figure snatched up the sword and stood over him. There was a grunt as the blade was pushed in, followed by a bubbling sigh. Then silence.

"Hold still," came a voice. There was a tugging at the bonds as the young man's hands and ankles were freed. "Can you stand?"

Flexing his wrists and feeling them for any blood, he said, "I think so." He paused. "Are they dead?"

"I should say they are. But let us be away quick."

He made a couple of attempts to get out of the chair. "What

took you so long to find me?" he asked, as he finally got his balance.

There was another soft laugh. "Do you know how many taverns there are on the river? I must have broken into ten before I found this one."

"Well, thank you, Ophelia. You were not a moment too soon."

"Next time, Robert, do not let yourself get taken so easily."

Chapter 2

Thomas Cromwell's study, Austin Friars, London
April 23, 1536

Thomas Cromwell pressed his fleshy fingers together and gave Robert Wychwoode an uncomfortable stare from beneath his black cap.

"What lessons have we learned from this near disaster?" he asked in a soft voice.

Robert cleared his throat and ran his fingers through his shoulder-length hair. "I should have told Ophelia and her brother Jasper exactly which taverns I was visiting in my search for the Spanish agitators."

"Precisely so," Cromwell said. "And perhaps sat with your back to the wall, rather than allowing those men to come up behind you?"

As Robert shifted uncomfortably in his chair, Cromwell turned to Ophelia.

"Now to you, Mistress Williams. Once again, you surprise me with your resource and ruthlessness. Two of our king's enemies lie dead by your hand." He raised an eyebrow at Jasper, Ophelia's tall, handsome older brother. "For a girl of but seventeen years, your sister has the courage of a man twice her age."

"And the skills, Master Secretary." Jasper gave her a warm look. "We have been making Ophelia do much practice with the knife, the sword, and moving in silence since you first engaged her after the Cornish rebellion. We have even instructed her in the use of her fists, so she might disable an opponent if she finds herself without a weapon."

"This has all been to great effect, I see." The corners of Cromwell's mouth twitched, in what Robert thought was the nearest the man ever got to smiling. Cromwell leaned forward. "What say you, Mistress Williams?"

"I did what had to be done, Master Secretary." She glanced at Robert. "Once Robert did not meet at the appointed time, I took it he had been captured." Her look of concern made Robert's heart give a small flutter. "Or killed," she added.

"Indeed." Cromwell nodded. "Which brings me to, let us say, the meat of this situation. The death of the Spaniards, welcome though it was, is not the end of the matter. There is still pressure from both Spain and the Papacy against the queen, whom they call a heretic. They sense her downfall is coming, since she was delivered of a stillborn and misshapen boy. The king fears God will not give him a male heir, at least not by this queen." He paused, looking at his three agents. "I tell you this in the strictest confidence, of course." They all nodded. "The Catholic factions therefore look to the queen's downfall as an opportunity to sow discord and sedition."

Cromwell stopped, and Robert held his breath. His master had the look of a man who is about to give the most important piece of information.

"The Spaniards were in part correct," Cromwell continued. "The king wants an annulment, then he will have Mistress Boleyn—as she will then be—sent to a nunnery. He wants rid of her." His expression hardened. "Which is why His Majesty has now charged me with finding just cause for her removal."

Robert let his breath out. "After he changed the religion of the land to marry her?"

Cromwell put his fingers together again. "Indeed."

Ophelia leaned forward. "Then what must we do?"

There was a silence, then Cromwell's mouth twitched. "You, Mistress Williams, will join her household. You have shown how you can assume a clandestine role, as you did in the guise of a nursemaid last year."

"What role?" Ophelia asked.

"A vacancy has arisen for a new lady-in-waiting." His dark eyes fixed on Ophelia's. "Elizabeth Browne, one of the queen's ladies, has just been dismissed following an accusation of loose living. Interestingly, upon her dismissal, she was heard to say that her guilt was small in comparison with that of the queen."

The three agents absorbed this. Then Robert pointed out the flaw. "Hearsay," he said. "The poorest kind of evidence."

"Precisely. Which is why Ophelia Williams will assume the vacant position and seek out hard evidence of the queen's guilt." He paused. "And when I told His Majesty of Elizabeth Browne's words, he was most clear that such evidence must be found." Cromwell paused, then added, "And if it were not, he said it would be my neck on the block."

There was an uneasy silence. Robert glanced at Ophelia and Jasper. The implication was clear. If Cromwell's neck was on the block, then so were theirs.

Chapter 3

Thomas Cromwell's study, Austin Friars, London
April 25, 1536

Ophelia stood back as Jeffrey Pritchett, Cromwell's master agent, pushed open the door and ushered her in. She took care to walk far enough into the room to accommodate the three-yard-long train that flowed out behind her.

Jasper and Robert stood up as she entered, their faces registering both surprise and delight at her appearance. Cromwell, however, stayed seated behind his desk, his black eyes giving nothing away.

After two days of preparation and a small army of tailors and women under Jeffrey's watchful eye, Ophelia was ready for the assignment.

Everything had been completed that morning; all the fittings done, alterations made and jewels found. Starting early, they had prepared her long blonde hair, combing and brushing it for what seemed like hours, then soaking it in warm water infused with rosemary and chamomile to give it a glossy shine. They had dried it with towels and brushed it again, before braiding and securing it with metal pins. A linen coif was fitted, ready for the French hood. Then she had been helped into a deep burgundy gown with a French-style square neckline edged in gold brocade, and a pair of full black velvet sleeves. One of the women had applied rouge to Ophelia's lips and kohl to her eyes, before another had secured the French hood with its gold gauze bordering. Finally, Jeffrey himself had placed two strings of pearls around her neck, plus a necklace with a gold cross pendant.

"This will pass?" Ophelia inquired, bestowing a small smile on Robert. She knew well enough that it would, for Jeffrey had been insistent on making sure everything was done to match Queen Anne's exacting standards.

"By all the Heavens, yes," Robert breathed, his eyes wide. This drew an amused glance from Jasper, under the lock of hair that habitually hung over his face.

"You are indeed a lady-in-waiting fit for a queen, my sister," Jasper observed.

"She will pass," Cromwell agreed. "Master Pritchett, please take us through the details of the scheme."

Jeffrey cleared his throat. "The plan is simple," he began. "Mistress Williams will be given a position in the queen's court, charged with finding evidence that can be used to have the marriage annulled. She will be masquerading as a lady by the name of Isabella Basset, who, in truth, does not exist, but who will be presented as having lived all her life secluded in Cornwall. This will not only avoid any difficult questions but allow Mistress Williams to talk of Cornwall with confidence. It is a place she knows well."

"A good plan," agreed Robert. "What say you, Ophelia?"

Ophelia gave him a small smile. "If the king wants his evidence, then I will do my best to find it."

"All the queen's ladies are vetted by her mother, Elizabeth Boleyn, Countess of Wiltshire," Jeffrey continued. "We have been briefing Ophelia on how to respond in an appropriate manner."

Ophelia gave a small shudder; the briefings had gone on for hours, taking her through every detail of Isabella's supposed past, and all the likely questions she would face from the queen's mother.

"Elizabeth Browne has already been dismissed from the queen's court," Jeffrey continued. "A replacement would be expected to be appointed immediately."

"Have no others been suggested?" Jasper asked, pushing the hair back from his face.

"Let us just say I have ensured there have not," Cromwell said quietly, making Ophelia wonder just what hardened tactics the secretary had used.

"And what if Ophelia is discovered?" This was Robert, with a worried frown.

Cromwell's mouth twitched. "Given Mistress Williams's recent exploits, I am confident she can look after herself. But—" he gave Robert a hard stare, "—you do raise a valid question, Master Wychwoode. Spaniard rogues are one thing, but she can hardly go around sticking her knife into courtiers." He turned his eyes on Ophelia. "That would not be a course of action I would recommend, Mistress Williams. Which is why Jeffrey will take on the role of a lowly kitchen servant, and be available to help if needed. You will report to him daily."

Ophelia glanced at Jeffrey. Today he was his usual well-groomed self; tall and assured. But she knew he was adept at taking on the most convincing disguises, from a dying street beggar to—who knew what other character? A lowly servant should be no problem for a man of his talents.

"And me and Jasper?" Robert asked.

"I see you two are both keen to be involved as well," Cromwell said. "To which end I have, ah—created—the need for two new palace guards. You will both be given suitable armour, and take up positions accordingly. Mistress Williams will have all our fates in her hand as she seeks the king's proof. We must do all we can to guarantee her safety."

Chapter 4

Early evening, Richmond Palace
April 25, 1536

The barge bumped gently against the jetty. A palace steward approached, flanked by two guards. "You have brought Isabella Basset?" he asked.

The coxswain nodded. The steward held out a hand to the nobly dressed lady seated in the stern of the barge, beside a fine-looking older gentleman. The gentleman stood and helped the lady step off the boat.

"Thank you, Father," she said as she smoothed down her skirts.

"Take good care, Isabella," the father replied. "This is indeed an honor—for you and for the family." He paused, giving the lady a steady look. "May God guide your tongue," he said, "so you speak the words that find favor with my lady of Wiltshire, and you secure the post."

"I pray He does, Father." She gave him a small curtsy.

The gentleman nodded, as if his job was done, then resumed his seat. He nodded to the coxswain. "Let us be off, good fellow."

As the barge pulled away, the lady said to the steward, "When am I to meet the countess?"

"Shortly, Mistress Basset. And then, should she believe you suitable for a post with the queen, you will be taken to the royal presence."

They walked ahead of the two guards, one of whom kept needing to push hair away from his eyes.

As soon as the barge rounded the bend and was out of sight of the palace, Jeffrey Pritchett asked the coxswain to land at a small jetty, where Cromwell was waiting.

"Mistress Williams is well delivered?" he asked.

"Aye, it went as planned. The steward has her in his keeping, ready for assessment by the queen's mother."

"Which will be a formality," Cromwell said. "As there are no other candidates."

"And Ophelia is well briefed," Jeffrey agreed.

Cromwell nodded, then his tone changed, becoming more decisive. "Now, Master Pritchett, you must change your garb and report for duty in the kitchens or you will be missed." He frowned for a moment. "The steward, he did not recognize you?"

Jeffrey chuckled. "I warrant not, Master Secretary. There is nothing to connect this—" he waved a hand down his fine mustard-yellow doublet, black velvet overgown, black cap and leather shoes, "—with the rough-hosed and tangle-bearded old fellow called Jenkin, who has been working in the palace kitchens as a porter these past three days."

Chapter 5

Three hours later, Richmond Palace
April 25, 1536

The meeting with the Countess of Wiltshire was over. Ophelia gave a sigh of relief as she sat back on the bed in the chamber she had been given. With a grunt of pleasure, she kicked off her tight shoes and wriggled her toes.

After studying Ophelia from every angle, the Countess had given a satisfied nod, and inquired of her skills with a needle. Ophelia answered honestly, using experience gained in her family homes in Salisbury and Cornwall under the stern eye of her older sister, Cressida. Next the Countess asked questions in both Latin and French, which Ophelia was able to answer in each language; the confidence again coming from her learning in the Williams's households.

All I have gleaned in my real life has qualified me as a Lady-in-Waiting to the queen, she thought. *Were my father higher in society, I might have been here in my own name!*

Then she gave a small gasp as a noise jumped unbidden into

her mind; it was the sickening sigh made by the Spaniard as she pushed the sword into his chest. *But in truth, you are no Lady; that life went behind you, Ophelia Williams, the day you were taken on as a spy by Master Cromwell. The day you became a killer for him. You are here to do a specific task—and that you must do.*

There was a knock on the door. She put on her shoes and stood. The steward, whom she now knew was called Robertson, entered and said, "Mistress Basset, you are to accompany me to the royal presence."

"Then I have secured the position?" she asked.

"That is not for me to say," Robertson answered with a look as if there was a bad smell beneath his nose. "Follow me."

Ophelia went with him down several passageways, until they came to a long room brightly lit by windows down the right side, with a large one at the far end.

"The presence chamber," Robertson said as he ushered her in.

She could just make out a group of women on a dais under the far window, although the light behind them meant they were hard to distinguish. Easier to see were the group of musicians standing halfway along on the left. They were talking amongst themselves, their lutes and viols held loosely.

Robertson swept off his cap and bowed low. "Mistress Isabella Basset, Madam," he announced.

A voice came down the room; loud, confident and clearly from someone of authority. "Bring her here. I do not see her clear."

Robertson straightened up and took Ophelia's arm, walking her up to the dais.

There were six ladies. Five were seated round the edges and one in the middle. The five all had their heads bowed over tambour frames with material stretched across, and were in the process of embroidering them with curved needles. As Ophelia approached, they all paused and looked up, giving her varying stares. Two seemed interested, two no more than curious—but the last one had a sneering look of disdain.

Yet it was the lady in the middle who demanded attention; from her dark hair with its severe parting under the pearl-edged French hood, to the gold chain at her neck with its B-shaped pendant and three iridescent drops below. She had no tambour on her lap; instead, a small dog was curled up, having its ears fondled by the lady's long, slim fingers.

Ophelia lifted her gaze to the face and felt her blood run cold. The small mouth was pursed in a look of stern disapproval, while the unblinking eyes that held hers were dark and hooded, giving an air of arrogance and power that she had scarcely seen before. Ophelia forced her gaze away. She dropped into a deep curtsy with her head bowed.

There was a yap and scrabble of claws on the floorboards, then the rustle of skirts as a pair of jeweled slippers stepped off the dais and into Ophelia's vision.

"Stand up, girl," said the voice.

Anne Boleyn stood marginally shorter than Ophelia, but the arrogant tilt of the queen's head meant their eyes were again locked.

"My mother tells me you will pass," the queen said. "And after the departure of the traitorous Elizabeth Browne, we are in need of another. You will start immediately, Mistress Basset."

"It is my pleasure, madam," Ophelia said. A gasp from the ladies on the dais made it clear that this had not been the right thing to say.

"Your pleasure?" the queen hissed, her dark eyes burning into Ophelia's. "Your pleasure? In truth, you are *honored*, I believe?"

"My... my apologies, madam," Ophelia stuttered. "I am truly honored."

The queen nodded, then went back to her seat, clapping her hands for the dog to resume its position. "The pleasure, I can assure you Mistress Basset, is all mine." As the dog jumped up, she continued, "And my pleasure, such as it may be, is to have total loyalty from you. I had to dismiss Elizabeth Browne for lacking the same; I trust I will not need to do this again?"

"Most assuredly not, Madam."

May God forgive me for the sin of lying.

"Disloyalty will be punished and with little mercy. Am I clear?"

"Perfectly, madam."

"Good." The queen indicated an empty chair directly behind hers, next to the lady who had sneered. "Sit."

Ophelia lifted her skirts and stepped onto the dais, conscious of everyone's stares—assessing her, judging her. *Well, I shall not be found wanting,* she thought as she sat. *Even though I serve a different master.*

Without turning, the queen said, "Margaret, hand Isabella your embroidery. She can take it on."

The one called Margaret said, "Madam, you are sure?"

After a stern look from the Queen, Margaret handed it over, then leaned across.

"Listen, girl," she hissed. "This is part of a gift from Her Majesty to the king. I have worked hard on this piece. I will check each and every stitch. If but a single one is out of place, in God's name, I will make you unpick the whole piece and start again."

The tambour frame held a cloth with the image of a garlanded Tudor rose. Half the image had been embroidered with tiny, precise stitches. Ophelia took a careful breath to calm her nerves, then picked up the needle and began to work.

"Mark," the queen called over to the musicians. "You will play for us."

Ophelia glanced up. One of the musicians was nodding, and Ophelia wondered why the queen was so familiar with such a man that she would use his given name only.

The music started, and Ophelia went back to her work.

Chapter 6

Midday, Richmond Palace
April 28, 1536

Ophelia glanced around several times as she approached the rough-planked door at the back of the kitchens. There did not seem to be anyone observing her. She positioned herself in the shadows behind the door and waited. A few moments later, there was the scuffing of a shoe, and a rough-looking kitchen servant peered round.

"Ophelia!" the servant whispered, wiping his hands on his grubby apron. "How goes it this day? Has the queen said aught that could have her in a nunnery?"

"This day is much like the others, Jeffrey," Ophelia replied in the same soft tone. "The queen remains the model of loyalty. We dress her in the morning and she says naught of interest in our cause; we sit with her all day long while she receives men on matters concerning her position as queen, and she says all she should; we sit with her at meals; we undress her and put her to bed in the evening, and still she says, or does, nothing untoward."

"We can do no more than stay attentive," Jeffrey observed with a shake of his head. "And you, Ophelia, how do you fare? Are you finding your place?"

"I have found friends, and seemingly made an enemy."

Ophelia gave a small sigh. "Margaret Coffin seems to have taken against me, for I can do no right by her."

Jeffrey raised an inquiring eyebrow.

"She made me complete some embroidery, and I did it to perfection. This seemed to upset her, almost as if she wanted me to fail so she could have me unpick the whole piece." She brightened. "But Mary Kingston and Elizabeth Somerset, the Countess of Worcester, seem most friendly, while Anne Shelton, the queen's aunt, and Elizabeth Stoner, appear to view me with only minor curiosity."

"Do naught to excite any concern among these ladies," Jeffrey advised. "Lest the mission is forced to end with naught of value."

She gave a small chuckle. "You should know me better, Jeffrey. For sure, I will not."

Ophelia ran softly around the palace, her long skirts clutched in her hand to stop them dragging on the gravel path. Arriving in the manicured gardens, she released them and slowed to a sedate walk. Almost immediately, there was the crunch of a foot on the path behind. Ophelia stiffened as Margaret Coffin came up alongside her, but she forced herself to keep walking. Was this just coincidence, or had the woman seen something?

"Mistress Basset," Margaret said in an overly casual tone. "Art well?"

"Quite well, thank you, Mistress Coffin."

The other woman had a small, almost triumphant, smile. "I note a slight redness of your cheek," Margaret said. "Almost as if you have exerted yourself by running. Am I mistaken?"

Ophelia walked on in silence, waiting to see where this might go.

"For 'tis strange," Margaret continued, her tone now becoming as triumphant as her smile. "I have noted you disappear while out for a walk at the same time each day. Why might that be?"

Again Ophelia said nothing, now trying to keep her breathing even. To keep her heart from racing. Then Margaret delivered her killer blow.

"And this very day," she whispered, "I decided to follow at a distance, and was surprised to observe you talking with a lowly serving man at the door to the kitchens."

Ophelia stopped on the path and faced Margaret, who continued, "What might that be about?"

Ophelia shook her head, trying to give nothing away.

"I think it is almost as if you were a spy, reporting to her master. Am I wrong?"

Ophelia's mind raced. Should she fell this woman with a single sharp blow from her fist, as Jasper had instructed her, then run to Jeffrey and have him get her out? It would mean the mission was unsuccessfully ended, putting her, Robert, and Jasper into the gravest danger. The queen would also know she was being spied upon, and her words on the subject could not be forgotten: *Disloyalty will be punished, and with little mercy. Am I clear?*

Ophelia decided to brazen it out.

"I fear you have misunderstood the situation, Mistress Coffin."

The other woman raised a disbelieving eyebrow, which Ophelia tried to ignore.

"I take my duty to the queen most seriously," she continued, "such that I wish to be assured that there is no chance of the food being prepared in the kitchens in a manner that might cause harm to her person. I have therefore sought a man to be my eyes and ears in that place." The eyebrow stayed up. "His name is Jenkin," Ophelia went on. "And he has agreed to report to me each day, such that I can be confident all is as it should be."

There was a long silence, with Margaret's mouth working as she weighed this up. Finally, she made a small nod. "Very well. While I find your tale quite incredible, especially for one so new to her position, I will accept it." She paused, then added, "For now."

Ophelia let out a slow breath, then nodded. "I am pleased you do, Mistress Coffin, for it is the truth."

God forgive me once again for a lie so easily given.

"Then go back to Her Majesty, and quickly. She is entertaining Sir Henry Norris and others of his party, and might be in need of your services. Go."

Forcing herself not to stumble on legs that now seemed unable to hold her weight, Ophelia started walking back towards the main palace building. She had gone no more than a few steps when there was a call from behind. She stopped.

"One more thing, Mistress Basset, if that is indeed your name."

Ophelia spun round, arranging her features into a look of concerned surprise.

Margaret was standing with her hands on her hips. "I am watching you, girl," she hissed. "Watching you close. You put a foot wrong— one foot—and it will be the worse for you. Am I clear?"

Ophelia did not trust herself to make a response. She turned on her heel and walked quickly away.

She hurried back to the palace, her legs still feeling as if they could scarcely carry her forward. After only three days, her position was perilous in the extreme; Margaret Coffin had as good as declared her a spy. It was but a matter of time until the queen was also informed. Then Ophelia would be cast out—or worse.

She needed to find the proof sought by Cromwell, and fast.

Coming into the royal apartments, she walked down the long passageway. She had just passed the slightly open door to the presence chamber at the far end, when a voice came from inside the room. The queen's voice.

"You have delayed your engagement for too long, Sir Henry," the queen was saying.

Ophelia glanced through the doorway but saw no person. The queen and whoever she was talking to, were out of view. Reasoning if she could not see them, then they would not see her either, Ophelia stopped to listen.

"If you stay any longer, she will not have you," the queen continued. "Perhaps she will make a different match."

"Madam, I prefer to tarry a time. I have not found the right moment to plight my troth."

"You must make the moment. That is your weakness."

"Do you call me weak, madam?"

"Would I be speaking the truth? I warrant it is so. You hesitate to declare to her your intentions." She paused. "Perhaps it is your feelings for me that govern your hesitation?"

"For you, madam?"

"You look for dead men's shoes," the queen said. "For if aught came to the king but good, you would look to have *me*."

There was a silence from Sir Henry Norris.

"Madam..." he stuttered eventually. "Madam, I..." There was the sound of a boot on the floor; he must have taken a step away from her. "I would *ne'er* dare to lift my head so high, lest I fear I would... I would *lose* it."

Ophelia turned away from the doorway, and leaned back against the wall. *If aught came to the king but good...*

Words that envisioned the death of the king.

That was treason. *Treason!* Uttered from the queen's own mouth!

Ophelia bit her lip. Now she had what Cromwell had needed—and so much more! He'd wanted something to justify an annulment; but this was *treason!*

Now to get word to Cromwell. She reached down and eased her shoes off before padding quickly back down the passageway.

This should have worked; her stockinged feet were making no noise on the polished wooden floor. If it were not for the single loose board that creaked loudly.

Ophelia froze for a second, glancing back at the door in horror.

It was flung open, and the queen appeared.

Ophelia turned and ran, ignoring the shout of "Stop, girl!"

Emerging outside, she hopped into each shoe, then picked up her skirts and ran on into the gardens.

The gravel path seemed to stretch on forever, threading its way between the various decorative knot gardens; each a square of trimmed hedges and herb borders in symmetrical shapes. Ophelia took a turn past one, heading for the kitchens. But before she had gone more than a few steps, there was a deep-voiced shout. A guard in a burnished breastplate and kettle helmet was closing in from the left. He was brandishing a wickedly tipped halberd. She looked to her right. Another guard was approaching from that side. As they closed in on her, she ran straight into the nearest knot garden. Clutching her skirts, she leapt over the low border hedge and stepped across the feature, her skirts dragging over the topiary. The guards yelled and circled round. They reached the far side together, just as Ophelia burst through before they could grasp at her.

There was a decorative arbor archway just ahead, with darkness beyond—suggesting denser trees and plants. Ophelia ran under the arch, and snapped a glance left and right. It seemed darker to the left, so she went that way.

Straight into the arms of another guard.

Chapter 7

Evening, Richmond Palace
April 28, 1536

The cellar was cold. Ophelia shivered, clutching her knees to her chest as best she could with her hands bound tightly together. A dim light came from an open casement with bars instead of glass, letting in the chill evening air.

There was a rattle of a key in the lock, and the door swung open. Her heart leapt when she saw it was Jeffrey, then fell again when a guard appeared behind him, shoving him brutally into the cellar. Jeffrey stumbled, falling heavily in front of her. That was when she saw the ropes binding his wrists and ankles.

And the blood down his face. And the black, puffy eye.

The door slammed, and they were together in the near-darkness.

"I am so sorry, Jeffrey," Ophelia said.

He rolled onto his side, then onto his bottom, and shuffled up to the wall beside her. "This is quite a turn of events," he said in a dry voice.

Ophelia was about to reply when the key turned again. The door creaked open and two guards came in, then stood on each side of the door, their halberds held forward. A moment later Steward Robertson came in with a lamp. Behind him, came two women.

It was the queen and Margaret Coffin.

The queen gave Ophelia a look of disgust, as if she were but a rotting carcass. Margaret, meanwhile, had a broad smile of triumph.

"I said, did I not, that I demanded loyalty?" the queen hissed. "Yet I find you listening at doors, and running away when challenged. Margaret here," she waved a hand at her lady, whose smile broadened even further, "tells me you concocted some cock-and-bull story of having this man spy for you in my kitchens. For my benefit." She gave a dismissive snort. "So I had him questioned."

The blood and black eye.

"And I now discover he is, as she first thought, another spy. Working for my enemies. Like you." The queen made a hollow laugh. "You are not long for this world, Isabella, or whatever might be your true name. You will need to make your peace with the Lord, but your fate will not be an eternity with Him. No, you must prepare to meet Satan instead."

Ophelia leaned forward. "You think silencing us will stop the truth being revealed?" she snarled. "That you are a traitor?"

The queen came closer and bent down. "Listen, you piece of carrion," she said, her face close to Ophelia's. "You are both here as spies. And spies can be disposed of, and no man is any the wiser." She stood back. "And spies who have knowledge of a conversation that could damage me in the eyes of my husband, the king?" She shook her head, as if in sorrow. "Such spies cannot be suffered to live."

"I knew you were a wrong one from the start," Margaret said.

"But I do have a proposition for you," the queen continued,

as if Margaret had not spoken. "Tell me who is your master in this enterprise, and I will make your deaths quick, and with minimal pain." She turned to the door, then stopped and looked back. "But if you would take your secret to hell, then your journey there will be slow—and painful beyond belief." She paused, as if to let that sink in, then said, "We will return for your decision in the morning. You have the night to decide the nature of your exit from this world."

She swept out, followed by Margaret. Steward Robertson paused by the guards.

"You two," he ordered. "Stay right outside this cellar and make sure no man—or woman—enters or leaves this night."

"Yes, Master Robertson," said one of the guards. Then all three men went out, the key was turned, and the prisoners were left in the dark.

Chapter 8

Early morning, Richmond Palace
April 29, 1536

The shout from outside the cellar jerked Ophelia awake. It was made by a voice that she did not recognize; yet it was brisk and had strong authority. "I care not for your orders, fellow; we have ours, and they are to search all the cellars."

There was a low rumble of the guard's reply, then the voice came again, "Listen, I have had word that agents of Spain have infiltrated this palace, and the fact you are standing guard outside this cellar leads me to suspect that you have them in here."

Another indistinct reply.

"If you do not open up immediately, I will see you forced-marched to Tyburn. Do I make myself clear?"

There was a short silence, then the key turned in the lock and the door creaked open. A man in the doublet, coat, and striped breeches of a senior army officer pushed his way in, followed by two of his men.

"Aha! Prisoners. My source gave correct information. A Spaniard I am told, masquerading as a servant, and his female accomplice, too." The man put a hand to his sword hilt. "What say you, fellow?"

"The señorita an' me," Jeffrey muttered, putting on a strong Spanish accent. "We are being hold here against our will, señor." Then he added, "The Spanish Ambassador; he will hear of this thing."

"What is that?" the soldier blustered. "The Spanish Ambassador? I think not, fellow. I have it on good authority that you will be taken to the first ship and sent back to Spain. Think yourself lucky you are not to be executed for spying." He turned to his men. "Untie them."

The two soldiers came forward, untied Ophelia and Jeffrey's bonds and pulled them to their feet. "Now, bring them out."

Ophelia and Jeffrey were marched out of the palace and into the bright morning sunshine. As she was pushed along by the soldier, Ophelia looked for the queen or Margaret, but neither was anywhere to be seen. Only Steward Robertson appeared, protesting weakly, but he was pushed aside by the officer.

A barge was waiting at the jetty. They were marched onto it and made to sit together at the back. The two soldiers then came round to the seat facing them.

As he sat, one of the soldiers pushed a lock of hair off his forehead.

Chapter 9

Thomas Cromwell's study, Austin Friars, London
May 19, 1536

Cromwell welcomed Ophelia and Robert into his study, and bade them be seated.

"You are to be congratulated, Master Wychwoode," Cromwell said, once wine had been poured and health inquiries made. "The idea to let it be known that a Spanish spy was being held was a stroke of brilliance."

"Thank you, Master Secretary," Robert said. "I knew you could not instigate a search yourself, for that would reveal that it was you behind Ophelia and Jeffrey's presence. I approached Sir John Seymour and told him I had it on strong evidence that a spy was being held. By the Lord's grace he believed me—I think because I suggested that the spy might be Spanish—and he sent a colonel with some men immediately. It was no trouble for Jasper and me to secure uniforms of the type worn by his men and slip in with the search party. Again, by God's grace, the colonel was loud enough that Jeffrey heard and pretended to be from Spain. The rest you know."

"I believe the success of your rescue of Ophelia gives you redemption after needing to be rescued yourself," Cromwell observed. "For otherwise we can be sure she and Master Pritchett would now be dead on Mistress Boleyn's order."

He turned to Ophelia. "I understand the Boleyn woman gave you the choice of my betrayal in return for an easier death?" He pursed his lips. "But then, you were rescued before the dilemma needed to be resolved. You were spared the choice, were you not?"

Ophelia stared down at her hands on her lap, finding it impossible to hold his eye. She could see what he wanted; to know what they would have decided. She looked up at Jeffrey standing by the fire. His eye was still darkened, but much less swollen. He gave her the smallest smile, and she returned an equally small nod. It was agreed between them. What was said in that dark cellar was their secret; one they would both keep to the grave.

Their conversation had gone on long into the night after the queen had left.

"She must know it was Cromwell who put us in place," Ophelia had said. "She only wants to have it confirmed."

"Belike," Jeffrey had agreed. "So what use is it for us to hold out? If she truly seeks our deaths, better for it to be quick and without any further pain. There has been enough already."

"Oh, come now, Jeffrey," Ophelia exclaimed. "I know they caused you harm to make you talk, but do not give up now."

"I have ne'er given up in all my life," Jeffrey said. "But I do ask, what is the purpose of enduring more pain—the greater pain of torture—when the alternative is altogether more preferable?"

"True, I suppose," Ophelia answered. "If the end is the same, maybe the easier path is the better one."

There was a long silence at this. Each lost in their own thoughts.

Torture—the very word made Ophelia feel sick to her stomach. What might the torture be? Might they cut her flesh? Screw her thumbs? Hang her to rot in a cage? Let the rats feed on her? Stretch her on a rack until her joints popped open? How long would she be left to die? And how greatly would she scream in agony and beg over and over for the sweetness of death?

Eventually Jeffrey said slowly, "I am sure if we were simply to confirm what she already suspects, then Master Secretary Cromwell would understand."

But... that would be a betrayal! It was what the queen wanted. How could they let her win? Surely the pain—however bad—was worth denying her the victory?

Ophelia took a deep breath. "No," she stated, with more confidence than she felt. "If I must go to the Lord's arms, then I would go with a clear conscience. I would not be a traitor. She must do her worst; I shall care not."

There was a long silence. Eventually Jeffrey's voice came from the dark.

"Then nor shall I."

"Now, to other matters," Cromwell said, his brisk voice bringing Ophelia back to the present. "The execution happened this morning at the Tower. Mistress Boleyn's body and head have been taken to St. Peter ad Vincula for burial. In an arrow chest, I believe."

Ophelia bit her lip. *How could she feel any sorrow for the woman's own downfall? After threatening her and Jeffrey with betrayal or torture?*

"Your information was the turning point in the case against Mistress Boleyn," Cromwell continued. "The words she spoke to Sir Henry Norris that day were indeed treason, especially when Norris confirmed them. And I believe Mistress Boleyn herself also confessed them to Sir William Kingston, the Constable of the Tower. But if you had not told us of them first, then we might never have known. For it seems self-evident that it was in neither Boleyn's, nor Norris's interests, to have volunteered the information."

"What of Margaret Coffin?" Ophelia asked.

Cromwell shrugged. "She has been sent back to her husband, but that is all. The woman is much chastened, and will not, I think, cause any more trouble."

Ophelia leaned forward. "It was because of her intervention that the queen was executed for treason, rather than being sent to a nunnery, as the King originally wanted."

"How so?"

"Because she stopped me to make one final threat in the garden. That meant I passed by the presence chamber at exactly the right moment to hear those words. Had she not, I would have passed by sooner. I would have heard nothing."

"Such a small thing, yet it will echo through history," Cromwell said. "A queen in all but name was executed today. I warrant an event of such import will ne'er happen again."

Author's Note

Everyone in this story, apart from the main characters (and the Steward Robertson), is real. Ophelia, Robert, Jasper and Jeffrey first "came to life" in my action adventure novel, *The Lawyer's Legacy*. In that book, I ended with Ophelia and Robert being offered the chance to work for Cromwell as "intelligencer" agents, and felt that they were interesting enough to see how this turned out for them. I feel they deserve a few more adventures, so I plan to write these over the next few years.

There really was a Margaret Coffin, although it is unlikely

she was as mean as I have made her—and for that I offer her my sincerest apologies!

Would Henry have really banished Anne Boleyn to a nunnery, or would he have wanted her executed from the start? There are arguments on both sides, so I have taken the view that the decision was for banishment, and that the (real) conversation between Anne and Sir Henry Norris being overheard, rather than being reported afterwards, was what swung Henry in favor of execution.

It might be a fictional "alternate history" rather than a "little known fact"—but I hope you enjoyed reading it as much as I enjoyed writing it.

ABIGAIL'S NECKLACE

ALINA RUBIN

St. Petersburg, Russia
1820

The tall magician, dressed in all black, tossed a handkerchief into the air. Midway through the flight, it disappeared. I assumed it was a handkerchief, but I couldn't see clearly, despite the candles in the enormous crystal chandelier illuminating the vast ballroom. My vision was marred for life after a bout of smallpox six years ago.

Important guests, elegantly dressed ladies and gentlemen, sat on sofas and chairs to watch the acts. Compared to their clothes, my concert gown of robin's-egg blue looked humble. A couple of spectators applauded the magician, but most were conversing amongst themselves.

The entertainers, Moishe and I among them, waited for our turn in an adjacent room where the air was thick with sweat and nerves. Dancers stretched their long limbs, singers warmed up their vocal cords, and I flexed and unflexed my wrists and fingers while watching the acts. So far there was a folk singer, a juggler who kept dropping his hoops, a puppeteer, and now, a magician. Only the singer impressed the viewers and me so far, but the performances distracted me from the queasiness in my stomach.

At twenty, I was too old to be awed by sleight of hand. I hoped, however, that the magician would put the guests into a pleasant mood, making them receptive to my and Moishe's performance. But so far, the sparse applause added to my anxiety. I didn't want to face a bored audience.

Someone touched my hand, and I spun around. A dancer in a calf-length skirt pointed to Moishe, who was tuning his violin in the back of the room.

"Who he to you? Husband?" She asked with a strong Russian accent and slightly lifted the ring finger of her right palm. The gesture confused me for a moment, then I remembered that the Russians wore their wedding bands on their right hand. She wasn't the first woman in St. Petersburg to subtly ask me about Moishe. He was tall, broad-shouldered, and slender, but what most people noticed was his confidence. This twenty-two-year-old son of a navy agent, away from Chatham for the first time, entered any ballroom in Europe as if he spent his whole life among the nobility.

I shook my head. "No. We are... music partners. But he's much better than me." I didn't feel like telling a stranger that Moishe's loving Jewish family adopted me when I was little, and we grew up together.

"Ah. But he likes you." The dancer winked.

I knew that, of course. A year ago, we almost wed. At that time, my heart was shattered, and I thought that marriage would mend it. Thankfully, we didn't go through with the wedding. I had to heal myself before I could love someone else. When Moishe invited me to join him in St. Petersburg as his accompanist, we agreed to treat each other as fellow musicians, caring friends, and nothing more.

Moishe came to stand by me. Wearing his black vest and overcoat in this stuffy room, he must have been sweltering. Sweat dampened his thick curls as he tugged his cream-colored cravat. My face perspired as well, and I was afraid that my carefully applied paste would run, revealing my ugly pox scars.

When the magician pulled a rose from his sleeve, Moishe whispered into my ear. "Who put this act before ours? Ordinary street magician. We'll be following his childish tricks with *Romeo and Juliet*."

"Perhaps we should play something more cheerful and fun?"

"No. We are artists, Abigail. Let them hear the most beautiful music we can play."

The magician raised his arms and said something in Russian. The spectators stopped their whispered conversation.

"Did you understand what he said?" I asked Moishe. He had spent a couple more months in Russia than me, and his father had taught him some of the language.

"I think he said that what he showed so far was to amuse the children, and now he'll demonstrate what he's capable of."

With a flourish, the magician bowed before a silver-haired woman in a tiara. He asked her a question, and she replied, shaking her head.

"He asked her to dance." Moishe translated for me. "She said that she hadn't danced for twenty years, and even before that, she was clumsy and regularly tripped over her feet."

The audience chortled but then grew quiet as the magician commanded something with a powerful voice. The woman rose. In a slow movement, she straightened her back and took two steps forward. Then she made a slow twirl with her hands up. The magician took her hand and spun her around the dance floor. When he bent her into a dip, a collective gasp came from the audience.

"She's a fine dancer. What's the point of this act?" I asked Moishe.

"I wonder..."

When she straightened, the magician snapped his fingers. As if awakened from a dream, the woman glanced around, then startled, and brought her hands to her face. The audience boomed and clamored for more. Several women were on their feet, waving their hands, trying to get the magician's attention. He bowed to thunderous applause.

My chin dropped. "He made her dance." What else could this man make people do?

Moishe snorted. "It's a trick. She's part of his act. I bet her gray hair is a wig."

"Oh, you are probably right." My shoulders fell. "I thought he had some kind of power over her. How silly of me."

The magician straightened and spoke. He said the word *hypnos* several times.

"What's *hypnos*?"

Moishe scratched his neck. "I'm guessing it means hypnosis or mesmerism. There is a German physician, Franz Anton Mesmer, who could put people into a trance, make them do various things, and even heal incurable maladies. But many of his claims were dismissed as quackery, from what I read."

An announcer came out and introduced our performance. At the sound of my name, my heart dropped, and my insides coiled. I clenched my stomach, breathing hard to suppress a moan.

Moishe's eyes narrowed. "Again?"

"It will pass."

The magician walked through the threshold past me. Then he turned on his heel and studied me.

"*Vam nuzhna pomosh?*"

I shook my head. "I'm sorry, I don't speak Russian."

"Do you need any help? You look like... you are ill."

His English impressed me. "I'm fine, thank you. I get nervous before performing. Stage fright." I forced a smile.

Moishe took my sweaty palm; his other hand grasped the violin.

"Are you sure you are all right?" he asked.

"Yes."

I kissed my mother's pearl necklace for luck. Running my fingers on the cool, smooth strand that rested above my collarbone sometimes ebbed my anxiety before performances.

When I was six, I wore it without permission to impress the girls who laughed at my patched dress. They stole it, and my mother never found the thief. Many years later, it was returned to me by our former landlady, who purchased it at the pawn shop. A rich woman saw me wear it and asked about my mother, who was dead by then. The woman turned out to be Mrs. Hearts, my godmother. But how my poor mother came to possess this extremely expensive necklace, each pearl a perfect tiny moon, was a mystery to me.

We came out into the center of the ballroom and bowed to the crowd. Their applause was eager and warm.

"*Anglichane.*" A woman in the front row whispered to her neighbor. Moishe told me that St. Petersburg's audiences loved anything foreign. Which was probably why Moishe's impresario sent him here to perform.

The woman who danced put on a monocle. "*Ona pohozha na pevitsu* Nellie Jones," she said to a young man next to her.

Did she just say my mother's name? I must've misheard her. It was impossible for her to know my mother, a mill worker and a cleaner, who died in poverty ten years ago.

I sat on the bench by the black pianoforte, then adjusted myself to reach the furthest keys. I'd spent an hour before the concert getting to know this instrument, feeling the weight of the keys, listening to the acoustics of the room. My fingers knew the music; I didn't need my eyes. I waited for Moishe to raise his bow and started playing an excerpt from *Romeo and Juliet*. As our instruments sang in harmony, I waited for my anxiety to melt away. Then I could float with the music, weightless and free.

Our fingers played each note without mistakes, yet my nerves refused to soothe. My throat was parched. My head throbbed. But the worst feeling was the gnawing in my belly. What did I eat or drink to upset my stomach like this? The ache grew worse by the minute.

Determined to push through the performance, I braced for Juliet's theme. The music wrenched my heart each time I played it, but it took all my skill to perform it as intended. Moishe's performance was technical perfection, each note clean and true. I was determined not to let my musical partner down. But this dizziness and pain...

A burning sensation crept up my throat. To keep it at bay, I arched my back and raised my eyes to the chandelier. It was spinning. The necklace felt hot and heavy on my neck, irritating my burning skin. Black spots danced in front of my eyes. My hands slipped from the keys.

Panicked, I rose on my shaking feet, looking for a way to run. In the next moment, my back and shoulders hit the marble floor, and the swaying chandelier was above my head. Dozens of voices shouted at once. Moishe's face loomed, and then the magician's eyes peered into mine. Like a blindfold, darkness covered my vision.

My eyes snapped open to a dim room, lit by a single candle. I squinted to discern where I was. A useless habit. All I saw were blurry outlines of a table, a chair and a bookcase.

I ran my fingers over the velvet fabric of the sofa I lay on. My head rested on a down pillow, and a heavy blanket covered my legs. Whoever brought me here wanted to ensure my comfort.

The air was heavy with smells that reminded me of a sickroom, like the one where I recovered from smallpox. Not the offending odors of vomit and blood, but the scents of alcohol, vinegar, and other medicinal ingredients. Was I ill? I touched my forehead. It was sweaty but cool. My belly churned with dull pain.

"Is anyone here?" I called.

"Abigail! How do you feel?" The concern in Moishe's voice made my heart race.

Heavy steps sounded, and two tall silhouettes entered the chamber. Moishe's curly head bent to me, while the other man lit two more candles on the table. Moishe was wearing his concert clothes. Only now my brain registered that I was wearing my blue dress. Earrings dangled from my earlobes, and my pearl necklace was clasped around my neck.

Moishe kneeled by me, and I grabbed his hand. "Where are we?"

Instead of answering, he swiveled his head to the man behind him, as if to ask a silent question.

"It's normal for her not to remember at first." The stranger's voice was low and rumbling and had a strong Russian accent. He stood too far for me to clearly see his face. I estimated his age to be around sixty, judging by his gray hair and his bent back.

"Miss Abigail Jones, my name is Pavel Gregorievich Chernov. Welcome to my home."

I shook my groggy head. "Why am I here, sir?"

"I've convinced Mr. Fridman to bring you here because my

skill may be of use to you. If you concentrate, you will recall the events of this evening."

My palms slid over the smooth pearls of my necklace. I must've worn it to play at a concert. My fingers throbbed with fatigue. I spent the day practicing at the hotel's pianoforte. We were to play at—

I bolted up to a sitting position. "Moishe, what time is it? We are to play at Prince Sokolov's palace."

At the thought of a performance, pain coiled my guts, and my stomach spasmed. My body curled into a fetal position. The necklace grew hot, burning my neck.

"It's happening again! Do something!" Moishe's voice cut through the pain.

Powerful hands laid me onto my back.

"What do you feel, Miss Jones? Tell me."

Instead of an answer, I moaned and clutched my middle.

"Close your eyes and count down from ten with me. Before we get to *one*, the pain will stop. Ten... Nine..."

A warm sensation spread around my abdomen. With each count, the pain diminished, and relief washed over me. When he said *one*, the stomachache was gone.

Memories of the evening flooded back. With apprehension, I opened my eyes. Chernov was standing over me, close enough to see his features. His eyes were squeezed, his hooked nose wrinkled, and his lips tightened into a line.

"You were that magician. But... this is not a trick. I do feel better."

Chernov nodded. "I'm glad to hear that."

"Thank you. But how did you make the pain go away?"

Before he could answer, Moishe spoke. "Abigail, if you are feeling better, let's return to our hotel. Then I will ask for a physician to examine you."

"Again?" Chernov threw up his hands. "I already explained.

The remedies the physician will prescribe will do her no good. Her pain is not from indigestion or closed bowels. It's from here." He pointed to his head.

I blinked rapidly. "What do you mean, sir? Are you saying my illness comes from the brain?"

"The mind." He tapped his forehead. "It stores memories. Sometimes we are afraid to remember, and the memory manifests through pain and illness. It's a condition that can be treated with hypnosis."

"Your hocus-pocus?" Moishe curled his lip and leaned away from Chernov. "No, we won't waste time on that. I'll take Abigail to the hotel and fetch a doctor."

Chernov spoke through his teeth with a forced restraint in his voice. "Without hypnosis, pain will return. She needs my treatment."

"Abigail, I'll order our carriage to be ready." Moishe made a move to go, but I caught his hand.

"Wait. I want to let Mr. Chernov work his... hypnosis on me. I want to know why I became ill."

I lay back down on the pillow and nodded to Chernov. His piercing gaze gave me chills, but I kept my voice even. "Please go ahead, sir. I'm ready."

Chernov cleared his throat. "Mr. Fridman, please sit in the chair by the wall. And not a word until I address you. You must not interfere."

Before moving away from me, Moishe squeezed my hand. "I'm still in the room, Abigail. I won't let him do anything to hurt you."

A warm feeling spread from my neck down. I didn't believe Chernov would hurt me, but it was nice to know that Moishe worried about me.

"The necklace you are wearing. How did you come by it?" Chernov asked.

"It was my mother's. The only thing I have left of hers."

"I can feel the energy coming from it." Chernov's voice was deep and soothing. "Close your eyes and breathe deeply."

My hands and legs became heavy as I filled my lungs with air.

"Imagine you are putting your pain away. You bundle it, put it in a woven basket and hide that basket in the farthest place of your home."

The modest flat, where I lived with my ma, appeared in my mind. I imagined myself stashing my pain under the bed where Ma and I slept.

"Where are you, Miss Jones?" Chernov's voice sounded close and far away at the same time.

The moldy smell of the tiny room filled my nose. "I'm at Churcham, where I lived with my ma until she died."

"What was your mother's name?"

"Nellie Jones."

"The necklace that was hers is now yours. Concentrate on it. What images does it bring?"

Another memory came, a recent one.

I stood in Mrs. Hearts's enormous home, next to the grand staircase. I was eighteen and wore my mother's necklace.

Mrs. Hearts pointed to the marble steps and spoke with her head down.

"Your mother held her heavy pregnant belly as she climbed the soapy stairs to help with the mopping. She slipped and fell to the bottom of the staircase. We thought that she was dead, but then she moaned and grabbed her belly. I ordered my butler to fetch the surgeon. You were born the same evening. It was a miracle that you and she survived. Later, Nellie asked me to attend your baptism. You are my goddaughter, Abigail."

"What did you see just now?"

"Mrs. Hearts telling me that she's my godmother."

"I sense your godmother will play an important role in your life. Now, think of your necklace. Let it reveal what you must remember."

I sank into the plush comfort of my bed, inside a room with a snow-white rug and gold-trimmed curtains. It was nothing like the tiny and cold flat where I lived with Ma.

Morning light streamed through the large window. Shouldn't I be up and helping Ma? I sat up, but the room spun. I reached for the cup by the bed. Warm milk relieved the dryness in my throat. There was a scone next to the cup, and I stuffed it into my mouth. The room stopped reeling.

The scent of jasmine perfume wafted in the air. A woman in a violet dress with a white lace collar walked in. My mother's pearl necklace decorated her long neck.

No! She cannot wear that necklace. It was Ma's!

The woman smiled at me, and her green eyes sparkled. "Don't be frightened, Abigail. This is your new home; your room. My name is Mrs. Hearts, but I want you to call me Mother. Did you like the milk and scones?"

"Where is Ma?"

"Scones are your favorite, right? And do you like your night-gown? I embroidered the flowers on it."

I stared at the pink nightgown that covered my arms and legs. It was the prettiest piece of clothing I've ever worn.

Mrs. Hearts took the cup from me and held my hand. Her own hands were soft like silk. Didn't she work with them? Or was she one of those women who pointed out to my mother where to dust or sweep?

"You've been very ill, Abigail. You still have ways to recover.

But now you are my little girl, and I will take great care of you. When you are better, you will run and play in your new home."

Where was *my* home? My and Ma's bed? My ma?!

"I want my ma!"

Mrs. Hearts winced as if she tasted vinegar.

"Nellie can't take care of you. You've almost starved to death, poor child. I've given her money, and she returned to that hole she lives in, leaving you with me. To be my precious little daughter. Do you understand?"

I shook my head.

She pointed to the pearls on her neck. "See, she gave her necklace to me. She insisted I show it to you, so you understand that I'm your mother now. If you want, I'll give it to you when you're a little older. It's not a plaything for a four-year-old girl. I'll give you many other trinkets to play with instead. My daughter Amelia has no use for them. But you and I will play all day, just like I used to when Amelia was little."

My lips trembled. "Ma? I want Ma!"

She crossed her arms. "How many times do I need to tell you? *I* will be your mother. You will also have a father and an older sister. You won't see much of them. They barely spend any time with me." She cringed. "But you won't be lonely at all. Besides me, you will have a nurse, a tutor, and a household full of other servants."

My tears poured like a flood. I wanted my ma. Her soiled dress. Her faded bonnet. I wanted to be hugged by her thin arms, kissed by her cracked lips. "Noo! I want Ma!"

She waved her finger in front of my nose. "You are being naughty. Hurting my feelings. I've done so much for you and Nellie. Now say that you are sorry."

"Abigail!" My mother flew into the room and wrapped me in a mighty embrace. "Don't cry. We're going home."

Mrs. Hearts stomped her foot. "Why are you here, Nellie? We had an agreement."

"It won't work." My mother planted kisses on my head. "She's my daughter."

An unladylike growl escaped Mrs. Hearts's throat. "It would've worked if you'd left her here when she was born, like I offered. But it's not too late. She's only four. She will forget you."

Ma lifted me into her arms. Tears streamed down her face. "I can't live without her."

I hugged my mother's neck and rested my head on her shoulder. My nose filled with her scent of sweat and dirt. Nothing in the world smelled better. I touched her wet cheeks and wiped them with my palms. "Don't cry, Ma."

A sigh rocked Mrs. Hearts's chest. "What would I give for someone to dry my tears. I'm married and have a daughter of my own. I have the biggest house in town, servants, carriages. Yet I cry alone into my pillow."

I wrapped my tiny hands around my mother's shoulder. "I want to go home."

"Yes. We are going home." My mother's nose touched mine.

"Nellie, take your necklace back." Mrs. Hearts sighed. When my mother approached her, she dangled the pearls in front of her. "It's the second time you've lifted my hopes and snatched them away. That hurts."

My mother took the necklace and stuffed it into her pocket. Her gaze dipped to her ripped shoes. "I'm sorry. I'm grateful for all you did. But I won't seek your help again. I've taken a job at the mill and cleaning homes in the evenings. That should pay enough to provide for the two of us."

Mrs. Hearts shook her head. "What happened to you? Why do you work such jobs? I finally remembered where I heard your name before. Five years ago, I saw your performance when you sang in London. You had me spellbound with your majestic voice."

"My majestic voice?" My mother threw her head back and gave a throaty laugh. "It's gone! Ruined."

Mrs. Hearts brought her hand to her lips. "Goodness. What a shame."

"There's nothing left of that voice." My mother glowered into Mrs. Hearts's wide eyes. "I don't want Abigail to know about my past. She's a daughter of a simple working woman."

"But you were—"

"No!" My mother grabbed Mrs. Hearts's hand. "Promise that if something ever happens to me, you won't tell her." She glared at Mrs. Hearts until the other woman bobbed her head.

"As you wish, Nellie. I promise."

"Abigail, open your eyes." Chernov's voice tugged me out of my mother's arms into the cold room where I had fallen asleep on his old sofa. Moishe slumped his head as he dozed on the chair.

Chernov peered at me. "You can sit up, but slowly."

I sat, and he walked around the sofa to stand in front of me.

"What did you see?"

I clutched my necklace. "I was four years old and starving, and my mother almost left me with my wealthy godmother. But then my mother returned and took me back." I wanted to be in her arms again. And to tell her she was the best mother in the world.

"What else?"

Moishe raised his head and yawned. "Abigail?" He jumped to his feet and sped toward me. "Are you all right?"

I raised my arms and stretched my shoulders. "I'm fine. Tired, confused, but not in pain."

"Then we can go?" Moishe offered me his hand to stand.

Chernov grunted and shook his head. "So impatient. Miss Jones has more to remember. Let her speak."

I furrowed my brow, struggling to recall my dream. "Mrs. Hearts said that my mother had a magnificent voice. And my mother answered that it was gone."

"Your mother was a singer? That makes sense." Moishe perched on the sofa. "I always wondered if your parents were musicians. My father taught you to play pianoforte, but you displayed natural ability even earlier."

"She didn't want me to know she was a singer. I wonder why."

Chernov took a few steps around the room then turned to me. "You became ill here in St. Petersburg, as you played a concert. Perhaps your mother performed in this city."

I tried to imagine my mother singing in front of people. She would be beautiful in a fancy dress and with her hair up. Was she famous? Did she travel? I could hardly believe it.

"What I saw—was it a dream? Or a childhood memory?"

Chernov shrugged. "A bit of both, perhaps. Young children repress the memories that scare and confuse them. Agony of hunger. Despair at being separated from your mother. Fear of another woman trying to take her place. Confusion about the revelation that your mother was once a singer. Your developing mind tucked that memory away, but your body remembered the pain. Stage fright, which may be connected to your mother's past, triggered the illness. Now that you have revisited your memories, you can make sense of them and absorb them into the story of your life."

I ran my hands over my abdomen. "Is the pain gone for good?"

"I'm afraid it will return." Chernov scratched his pointed chin. "Your treatment is not complete."

"Yes, it is." Moishe jumped to his feet. "Enough of this nonsense. Abigail needs a knowledgeable physician."

Chernov sighed and bowed to me. "Miss Jones, you are welcome to visit me again. I won't charge you for today. And please continue wearing your necklace. It will help you remember. *Do svidania.*"

I leaned on Moishe as he led me into the cool night air and helped me into the carriage.

The next morning, I was in the hotel's music room, practicing. It was my requirement of our impresario to stay only in places that had a pianoforte available for me to rehearse at any hour. That's probably why we received rooms at the best hotel in St. Petersburg and not some second-rate inn.

My body was surprisingly energetic after only a few hours of sleep. The light breakfast of buckwheat *kasha* that my maid Olga insisted on feeding me, settled in my stomach. My fingers were warmed up to play, but my mind was not on the music. It was buzzing with questions about my mother. Was she once a great singer? What happened to her?

I closed my eyes, ran my hands over the necklace, and remembered my mother. She sang lullabies to my baby brother and sister. Her voice was weak, hoarse. Coughs interrupted her singing. Perhaps her lungs were damaged before she caught the pneumonia that killed her. Until her death, she toiled, humming melodies as she mopped the floors or worked the machinery at the textile mill. What did she hum? I could almost hear the sorrowful melody.

La-la-la-la, pap-pap-pam-pam-pam.

Pressing various keys, I searched for the right notes. Moishe excelled at playing by ear and could've helped me, but he left early to speak to our impresario about cutting our tour short if needed and returning to England. He also wanted to inquire about a physician we could consult in St. Petersburg. I wanted to believe that his worries were unnecessary.

After a painstaking hour, I finally found my mother's melody. Elated, I played it, hearing my mother humming the song as she scrubbed floors on her hands and knees.

A rich baritone sang behind me: "*I letom i zimoi slepaya. Podaite zh milostinu ei.*"

My hands froze on the keys. The voice sang the words to the music I was playing. With my jaw hanging open, I turned. A tall man with streaks of silver in his black hair, dressed elegantly in a dark navy tailcoat, stood behind me, next to a gray-haired woman in an emerald-green dress. Despite my poor vision, I was sure she was the same woman who danced with the hypnotist last night. Her lilac perfume floated in the air.

"Why did you stop?" The man asked in almost flawless English. "I was getting to my favorite part."

I rose and folded my hands, as if in prayer. "Please tell me what this song is. My mother knew it."

The man adjusted his golden cufflinks. "It's a piece I created for a British singer, Nellie Jones, twenty years ago. Miss Jones wanted an original song to win over the hearts of St. Petersburg's audiences. I translated a poem by Pierre-Jean de Béranger about a blind beggarwoman and put it to music."

"You are the composer?" I gaped.

"I'm Alexei Mihailovich Rogozov, a retired opera singer, and a music instructor. And this is the Countess Maria Vladimirovna Suvorova."

I trembled with excitement. "Nellie Jones was my mother. You wrote a song for her? She sang it here in St. Petersburg?"

He gave me a weak smile. "Here in Russia, a polite young lady would curtsy before a noblewoman and only then ask questions."

"I'm sorry." I made a deep curtsy before Countess Maria. "I'm so overwhelmed that I forgot my manners. And I didn't expect a countess to visit. If she had sent for me, I would have come right away."

Rogozov translated for me, and Countess Maria waved her hand in dismissal and smiled as she replied.

"She said that it's a beautiful day and she enjoys walking by Neva. When I came today to give her granddaughter a singing lesson, she sent her to play outside instead and invited me to accompany her on this visit. Besides, she wasn't sure that you were well enough to see her. You fainted yesterday at the concert?"

I nodded. "Yes, but I'm better. Please tell me all you remember about my mother. She died of pneumonia when I was ten years old. I knew nothing about her past as a singer."

When I mentioned my mother's death, Rogozov's shoulders fell. He translated my words to Countess Maria, who touched her cheek. Then she opened her arms for an embrace. Despite having met her only minutes ago, I felt the warmth of her hug.

With a wistful expression, Countess Maria removed a rolled up, yellowish paper from her satchel. She unfolded it and pointed to something on it. I brought it to my face to read. The print was in Russian, except for one name—Nellie Jones.

"Her name wasn't translated to emphasize that she is English, which made her intriguing to St. Petersburg's audience. This is a program from Bolshoi Kamenny Theatre, from her last concert here," Rogozov explained.

My eyes went wide. Questions flew off my tongue with

many more pressing on my mind. "What did she sing? What did she wear? Why was it her last concert?"

Countess Maria grinned at me and went over to the sofa, gesturing for us to join her. When I sat next to her, she put on her monocle and peered into my face before saying something to Rogozov.

"She says that you have an uncanny resemblance to your mother, except—except you are even more striking."

Heat rose to my face, and I covered my cheeks with my hands. "I'm sure it's not what she said. I may resemble my mother, but her face wasn't marred with pox scars. I cover them with paste before performances."

The countess said something and pointed to a round mole on her face. Then, to my shock, she peeled it off, revealing a faded scar.

Rogozov leaned in. "She had smallpox in her youth. The illness killed her beloved brother. She says you are beautiful. A survivor."

"Thank you." I squeezed the countess' hand. "Please tell me about my mother."

Her lips curved into a nostalgic smile, and she spoke with animated gestures.

"Twenty years ago," Rogozov translated, "the countess sat in her box in the Bolshoi Kamenny Theatre. She came to listen to the young British singer Nellie Jones, who was quickly making a name for herself. After arias in English, French, and Italian, Miss Jones took everyone by surprise by performing a soulful Russian song, the one you were playing when we came in. That song told the story of a once-famous and beautiful performer, crippled and blinded by illness, who was then reduced to begging. At the end of the song, Miss Jones fell on her knees, pleading for charity toward the heroine of the song. That performance moved Countess Maria to tears. She invited Miss Jones to her box and asked her to give a private concert at her salon. They communicated in French, a language your mother spoke well."

I wanted to pinch myself to be sure I wasn't dreaming.

Rogozov exhaled a long breath. "I was at the theater as well. I was extremely proud of Miss Jones for mastering the song and performing it with such feeling. She was better than at our frequent rehearsals." He stared down, and his fingers tugged on a gold button. "I wish I had spoken to her after the performance and told her how wonderfully she had done. I could not have known it was the last time I would see her."

Countess Maria smoothed her dress. Her lips turned down, and her breath hitched. Anticipating a turn in the story, I shifted to the edge of my seat.

"Three weeks later, the countess was entertaining her guests at her salon. Miss Jones was two hours late, and the hostess feared she wouldn't show at all. Rumor had it that she had cancelled other private concerts and social gatherings. Some said she was ill; others whispered about a romance." Rogozov paused and scratched his chin. "She also stopped her rehearsals with me. Her note to me was polite and appreciative but offered no explanation as to why she wasn't interested in further lessons. I'm ashamed to say I took offense and didn't follow up. I wasn't there the evening she came to sing for Countess Maria and her friends."

The portly, bold Maître d'hôtel walked in and bowed before the countess. His tone was apologetic. When she replied with a smile, he kissed her hand. Then he addressed me in English.

"You should have warned me that you were expecting distinguished guests. I would have greeted them earlier and arranged for refreshments. The countess asked for tea with honey and lemon for herself and *Gospodin* Rogozov. Would you like the same?"

"I'd like my tea with milk, please."

He scoffed, then nodded. "As you prefer." Despite his fancy French title, he didn't bother showing politeness to an unknown British musician.

When he left, Rogozov grinned at me. "Nellie—I mean Miss Jones—also liked her tea with milk. She told me that's how most people in England drink it. It was before I traveled around Europe, and her words took me by surprise. I tried to convince her that a singer should drink tea with honey and lemon to soothe her throat, but she refused to change her habit. She said it was a small pleasure that reminded her of her home."

Exactly how I felt when I sipped tea with milk and gazed out of the window in my hotel room, seeing the gorgeous but unfamiliar city. "Was she homesick?"

Where was her home before she came to St. Petersburg? Who taught her to sing? There was so much I didn't know.

"I believe she missed England." Rogozov tilted his head. "Touring is exciting, but most performers at some point long for the comfort of their homes. They crave familiar food, and pine for their families or close friends. And when people fall ill in a foreign country, many promptly return home."

I swallowed, thinking of Moishe arranging for our return to England. "Is that what happened to my mother?"

His gaze shifted to the countess, who folded her hands at her chest as she spoke. When she finished, she touched my arm.

"When the hostess was ready to give up on waiting, Miss Jones finally arrived. Alone, without an accompanist. Her cheeks were flushed, and she trembled in her fur coat despite the heat from the fireplace. Countess Maria sat her down in the antechamber, asked a maid to fetch some water, and told Miss Jones she would apologize to the guests on her behalf. Miss Jones threw her coat on the floor and rushed into the sitting room. 'I will sing *The Beggarwoman*. Please listen to the lesson the song teaches,' she announced before she started."

Two maids set the silver trays with tea and a plate of Russian sweets, *pechenia* and *prianiki,* not unlike sugar and gingerbread biscuits, with raspberry jam in a crystal bowl. Countess Maria sipped her tea and spoke. I waited for her to finish before relieving my thirst.

Rogozov finished chewing his *prianik* and translated. "After singing the first line, Miss Jones had a coughing fit. After gulping a glass of water, she tried again. Her singing was screechy and hoarse, painful to hear. The audience cringed. When the moment came to belt out a high note, her voice, so powerful and rich only weeks ago, cracked. Guests snickered and huffed, and a few men whistled. Miss Jones burst into tears, and before the countess could stop her, ran out of the room and then out of the house, forgetting her coat. The doorman chased her for a couple of streets with that coat and caught up with her only when she slipped and fell onto the snow."

"Oh dear!" Ice ran down my veins. "How horrible."

"He helped her up, wrapped her in her furs, and found a coach to take her to her lodging." Rogozov's voice was slow and melancholic. "He returned and told all this to the senior servant, who in turn informed his mistress. Concerned, Countess Maria decided to send her physician and a maid skilled in nursing to Miss Jones. It was a fateful decision. They found her tossing on her bed in delirium, all alone. Her servants had fled. When the countess' maid returned two weeks later, she said that Miss Jones suffered from influenza, and it took all her and the doctor's skill to heal her. The singer was finally out of danger and sent thanks to the countess for her lifesaving intervention. And we wonder if they saved not one but two lives. When were you born?"

"Right before Christmas of 1799."

Rogozov pointed to the date on the program. "March 1st of 1799. The private concert for Countess Maria's salon was three weeks later. It's possible that when your mother fell ill, she was pregnant with you. Too early for her and her caregivers to know."

My head reeled, and I slumped onto the sofa. I might've been conceived in St. Petersburg during my mother's performance tour. I knew nothing about my father. My mother never spoke of him, and I was too shy to ask Rogozov or Countess Maria if they knew who he was.

When the room stopped swaying, I shook myself. "I thank you for saving my mother's life that day. Her fate was tragic. She lost her voice. Worked at the mill and as a cleaner to make a living. But she was a loving mother to me and to my younger brother and sister."

Countess Maria cupped my face and kissed me on both cheeks before she spoke again.

"We are overjoyed to meet her daughter, also a musician. The countess wonders if you can sing as well as you can play the pianoforte," Rogozov translated.

"Oh no, I cannot sing. Not well, anyway." As the words flew from my tongue, a warm sensation spread from my neck, like my mother's embrace. "But I want to learn the song my mother performed, about the blind beggar. When my mother died, I begged for money to survive. And later I caught smallpox, which marred my vision."

Rogozov and Countess Maria conversed with vigorous gestures. "It would be my privilege to teach you in memory of your mother, free of charge," Rogozov said. "Countess Maria is having a gathering at her salon in two weeks. She wants you to perform for her guests. If you work hard, two weeks should be enough for you to master that song."

"Sing in front of an audience?" My hands went to my belly, anticipating its churning. "No, I can't."

"Stage fright? We will work on that." Rogozov winked at me. "When I was starting out, my stage fright was so severe I needed help from a hypnotist to conquer it. There's one in St. Petersburg."

"Chernov. I met him yesterday. Yes, I think I will need his assistance."

The countess patted my hand and stood. When I rose, she hugged me again and touched my necklace. "*Ot Mami?*"

"Yes." I smiled. "It was my mother's."

Countess Maria beamed and said something.

"She said your mother wore it when she performed."

Rogozov led the countess to the front door. I followed, caressing my pearls.

The doorman bowed and swung the door open for the countess. She said something to him, while Rogozov turned to me. His eyes scrutinized me, and my back stiffened. "I will return here at six o'clock for your first lesson. By that time, you must eat a bowl of hot soup, take a brisk walk for at least half-hour outside while wearing a proper coat and a scarf, and have an afternoon nap."

My mouth hung open as I processed Rogozov's instructions. Eat hot soup? Nap? Is that required of a singer?

Moishe walked through the door, bumping Rogozov with his shoulder. Rogozov ignored his apology, his eyes fixed on me.

"Why do you gape like that, Miss Jones? Singing requires serious exertion and discipline, and caring for your body is vital. I don't allow my students to swoon." He shook his finger at me before he left.

"Who was that?" Moishe stammered, staring after Rogozov.

"My new music teacher." I shifted my feet. "Moishe, why don't you wait for me here? I'll put on my coat and a scarf, and we can walk together. There's something we need to discuss."

He checked his pocket watch. "Are you sure you are well enough to walk? I arranged for a doctor to see you. He's coming at six o'clock. And before that, I was hoping to show you a piece

I was working on. The violin part is perfect for my skill, and the pianoforte accompaniment is simple. You'll be able to handle it."

My mother's necklace warmed my neck, making my heart pump.

"Moishe, I'm sorry. I can't see the doctor at six. That's the time of my music lesson."

He knitted his brow. "What lesson?"

"I'm only a mediocre accompanist. I don't have the talent to be a soloist on the pianoforte. And I have stage fright. But perhaps it's because I was training on the wrong instrument."

"But what about our plans? The tour, and after that?"

I touched his cheek. "Moishe, my mother was a singer. I need to know if I can learn to sing. That man you saw, Rogozov, can help me. I will also need Chernov to help me get over my stage fright. Perhaps hypnosis will reveal more memories of my mother. Or even my father. I will finish the tour with you, but after that, I must commit myself to working on my voice."

He swayed on his feet, then dropped his head. "Let's take a walk."

Inhale. One, two, three. I did a breathing exercise Chernov taught me. *Hold your breath. One, two, three.*

My fingers ran through my necklace. *When you touch your necklace, your mother will be with you,* Chernov told me at our last session. *She will help you through your performance.*

I sat next to Rogozov, in the corner of an intimate sitting room of the Countess Maria's palace, with twenty people or so listening to Moishe play. Several of the guests had approached me earlier and told me that they remembered my mother, that I look like her, that they were saddened to hear of her death, and that they were glad to see me. Some wore a guilty expression; perhaps they regretted their behavior the night my mother sang for the last time. Hearing them talk of my mother's flawless voice and powerful stage presence was a surreal experience.

My mother must have been devastated to lose her ability to sing. It's no wonder she fled to her homeland and chose to live in humble obscurity. Perhaps the illness affected other functions, such as her memory or concentration, and that's why she could only work simple jobs. When she fled Russia, she left behind everything that reminded her of her life as a performer, except for two small things: her pearl necklace, and the baby that was growing in her womb.

Twenty years later, I sat in the same room where my mother had last performed. Rogozov told me that I inherited the rich timbre of my mother's voice. I wanted to prove to myself that I had her spirit.

The melody of Moishe's violin flowed and rippled. His playing was technically superb as usual, but I sensed a new depth of emotion in the music. He sounded... vulnerable. My triumph tonight could lead to us going our separate ways for a while. He would continue with other cities on the tour, while I would keep working with Rogozov on my singing.

Moishe finished playing and bowed to enthusiastic applause.

"Are you ready?" Rogozov whispered into my ear. When I nodded, he took my hand and ushered me to the middle of the room. This time, I didn't shake on my feet or wince from a stomachache. My heart danced in my chest, and I beamed at the excited audience. They wanted me to succeed. I couldn't fail them, or our generous hostess Countess Maria, or my diligent teacher Rogozov. Or Chernov, who taught me how to control my stage fright. Or Moishe, who put away his pride and came tonight. Or my mother, who inspired me. Or myself, after I'd poured my heart and soul into mastering the challenging song.

Rogozov introduced me, and I caught my mother's name in his short speech. Yes, I was my mother's daughter. I would pick up where she left off. After he finished speaking, he clapped me on the back, reminding me to keep a tall spine. Then he nodded to Moishe, who came to sit by the pianoforte. Today, he would play the accompaniment for me.

I ran my fingers over the smooth pearls of my necklace.

Always remember why you sing, Abigail.

Where did those words in my head come from? The voice sounded like Ma's. My heart lifted. I smiled at Moishe, who was waiting for my signal to start, and mouthed *thank you*. In my heart I added, *I will miss you*. We would go our separate ways after the tour. Our parting was necessary for his musical career to flourish and for me to find my voice.

I focused on the audience. Even though their faces were a blur, I felt their affection and made my voice strong and crisp. "Twenty years ago, a British singer, Nellie Jones, came to sing here. She chose a song that teaches an important lesson. Fame, beauty, fortune, and, unfortunately, health, are fleeting. Please be kind and feed a beggar, check on a friend, and give someone a second chance. A small thing like a coin, a kind word, a minute of your time, can make the difference between life and death."

Rogozov translated, and the applause echoed through the room. After kissing my necklace, I began to sing.

Author's Note

"A small thing like a coin, a kind word, a minute of your time, can make a difference between life and death." While the necklace connected Abigail to her mother and inspired her to sing, it also revealed an act of kindness that saved her mother's and Abigail's lives.

The poem *La Pauvre Femme* by Pierre-Jean de Béranger was written in the early 1800s. It became a popular Russian song (*romance*) later in the century with music by Alexander Alyabyev. There were several translations, the best known is by Dmitry Lenskiy. When I imagine Abigail's performance, it sounds like the one by Polina Konkina, except in a 19th century sitting room of a palace and not on the reality show Golos/The Voice.

The term for hypnosis in England of the 1820s was "animal magnetism" or "mesmerism," named after the German doctor Franz Anton Mesmer. I chose "hypnosis" for modern readers.

If you wish to follow the characters of this story, enjoy the Hearts and Harmony series by Alina Rubin. The first book, *Abigail's Song*, was the Chanticleer Grand Prize Winner of the Goethe Award in Late Historical Fiction 2024.

P.S. In *Abigail's Song*, Mrs. Hearts says she gave the necklace to Nellie at Abigail's baptism. For this story, I reimagined that the necklace had belonged to Nellie before Abigail's birth.

A HOUSE OF SALT

VANITHA SANKARAN

Coimbatore, Tamil Nadu
October, 1942

The clatter of looms in Thama's family home drowned out the Elders' voices. Colloquially called *Thari Veedu*, the family weaving house never rested. Not anymore. Spindles spun, looms thudded, and hands worked thread over thread to keep up with British demands to supply a war effort on another continent. The once-familiar smells of cotton dust and boiled starch no longer soothed Thama. They hadn't since the Mahatma's calls for *swaraj*—self-rule—and not since her father had left months ago to serve as a *khansama*, a house steward, in a stately manor commandeered by a British official in the fancy district of R.S. Puram.

Gandhi-ji's formation of the Quit India independence movement, only two months ago, had landed the leader in jail, but that only served to inflame the freedom fighters. Protests, boycotts, and violence against government buildings erupted across the country. The British responded with ruthless force, their punishments swift and severe.

Still, the rebellion continued.

Tonight, the discussion next door concerned everything Thama craved hearing: news of the cotton industry's resistance attempts; word on how the Mahatma fared; and especially anything that might bring her father back to his weaver roots and away from his life as a spy. He hadn't been home for months now; hadn't returned even for her twelfth birthday. People in this community knew her father by the softness of his thread. The firmness of his cloth. Now, far from home, he answered to a stranger's name, serving English tea and collecting English secrets.

Like his brothers, he believed independence from the British was not only possible but inevitable. Unlike them, he risked his very life to see that dream fulfilled.

The discussion next door grew heated. Plucking at tiny bits of thread still clinging to her heddle, Thama strained to hear more. She only caught snippets. Like:

Obaidullah has been taken. A Congress leader and storied freedom fighter.

How do they still expect us to weave for the war? The British had decimated their local industry. Every man and woman in their compound worried over whether they could scrape together enough rupees for rice and vegetables to eat the next day.

If we strike now, we must strike hard. If? Had they not heard Gandhi-ji's call? Had they forgotten how much had already been taken?

Did they not parrot Gandhi's own words? *Spin for freedom, weave for* swaraj. *Our cloth, our salt, our land must be returned to us.*

Did they not have pamphlets posted up in this very compound, ones that exhorted them to act? *Let no British cloth cover your skin, no taxed salt touch your tongue, no silence steal your voice.*

No, they could not suffer living under the thumb of this faraway British king any longer.

A point her uncle made swiftly. The other men fell into line, and the conversation shifted to acts of sabotage that needed assigning. Underground missives. False records. Fake names for the British to waste time hounding.

Then the true strike came:

The police already suspect us. They are planning a surprise inspection. We need Arunachalam back. Her father. *If he's missing, they will know we are complicit.*

Thama almost abandoned her loom, but in the other room, her mother shouted first: "What if you call him back and lead the British straight to him?"

Her uncle held firm. "My brother volunteered for this post. He knew the risks. To himself and to us."

Thama strained to glean anything from the yells of voices that responded, all men, all talking about things like wartime and sacrifices and leaders.

Her grandmother sliced through the noise. "What are you lingering over, girl? Stop dithering over your loom and go fetch me some thread."

She obeyed out of practice as much as surprise, darting between bundles of carded cotton and sacks of dyed yarn, her bare feet slapping against the packed earth floor.

If her father served as the head of their small band of *pattunoolkarrar*—traditional silk weavers—now pledged to Gandhi-ji's mission, then his own mother served as the head of their family. Which meant Thama couldn't keep the woman waiting. She sorted through spools of thread collected in baskets near the spinning wheel and chose the fattest one.

Her grandmother took the spool with a critical grunt. "Slow hands make broken cloth, child. But restless ears break the mind." She waved a hand at the piles of woven cloth heaped on a nearby table. "Check the day's work."

Thama pulled off the top length of cotton fabric and dropped to the floor. She laid the cotton across her lap and traced its threads slowly, following the rhythm of warp and weft. Her fingers paused at a slight irregularity—just a breath of a shift in spacing—then moved on. She kept going, as if learning the cloth's quiet language, one thread at a time. Across the compound, her aunts and sisters and cousins kept up their work, looms creaking in measured harmony. The sounds of her home and her heritage stretched back across generations.

Still, like her, all the other women bent their heads and their ears toward the voices next door. How could they continue their work when their very world threatened to go up in flames?

Normally, Thama would try to guess who had woven a piece of cloth based on its tightness and types of errors. Her aunts and older cousins teased her for being so in tune with the cloth, jeering at her guesses, which proved correct more often than not. Tonight, though, she just folded this piece and moved on to the next.

Her grandmother eyed her critically; then looked around the room at the others. All of them tired. All of them training their eyes and ears and attention on the arguments resounding in the neighboring hall.

Fingers still moving across her loom, the older lady made an announcement. "Listen, I understand that each of you wants to be in the room next door. But with the British already increasing our quotas, we can't afford an evening off. So let me tell you what they are talking about. Raghunatha-*ayya* sent word. A secret inspection *is* coming. They're planning it for just before *Deepavali*—when everyone will be home."

The loom chamber went still. The British had long suspected weaving compounds of stockpiling their rough, hand-spun cloth—*khadi* cloth—for the resistance fighters. Every few months, a circular showed up in their home informing of one inspection or another. But one conducted in secret?

Valli Periamma, her father's older sister, clicked her tongue. "Another inspection? Don't they know every inspection sets us behind quota? That Kattai Pillai, simply shaking his tail for the British."

Thama's grandmother shot her daughter a look. "Mind your mouth, Valli. Whatever else Raghunatha-*ayya* is, at least he warned us. Others will not even do that much to help."

Thama's cousin Selvi didn't even look up from her bobbin. "You call that help? Deepavali is in two weeks only. Telling us at the last minute makes him seem friendly, but accomplishes nothing."

The other women added their own opinions, but Thama understood the threat her grandmother warned over: her father served as the head of this compound. If the British appeared and her father wasn't present, all of Thari Veedu would suffer. Their neighbors would suffer. Even Zamindar Raghunatha Pillai would suffer.

Through the thin wooden partition that separated the work-space from their living space, her mother's voice sharpened. "If my husband needs to return, then we need to send him word."

Thama froze, her breath catching.

Her uncle's answer came low, careful. "We cannot. You said it yourself: if the British suspect him, if we mention even one wrong word, we lead him straight into their trap. We'll say he's passed. That he's gone. It's safer."

Thama gasped. For a moment, it felt as if all the sound in the compound had been swallowed whole.

"They have taken so much from us. Our cloth, our salt, our

lives. If you declare him dead, he will never be able to return home. He is my husband, Thama's father—"

Her uncle's response sounded gentler this time. "He chose this, Meena. You know he did. When India is free, he can come home."

"If India ever wins freedom. If." Her mother's voice grew loud in anger. "Don't promise outcomes you cannot deliver."

Thama squeezed her hands into fists, pressing them against her lap.

Her grandmother must have noticed the tension in Thama's body because she sighed, shaking her head. "Your father is where he is needed."

Thama's throat burned. "And where am I needed?"

The old woman studied her for a long moment, then nodded toward the loom before them. "Here. With your hands, with your thread. Your mother worries, but she still weaves. That is how we fight." Her hands moved over the loom as she spoke, tightening the weft.

"This wasn't the first time, you know," she said, pausing. "My mother used to speak of the Chapati Movement, long before my time. A strange thing. Villagers passed chapatis from house to house, no markings, no messages—just warm bread wrapped in silence. But it spread like fire. The British never understood it. They thought they ruled our bodies. But they never ruled our knowing. That's what frightened them most."

Thama glanced at the fabric taking shape before her grandmother. The cloth stretched tight across the frame, each row of threads locked in place. Her grandmother wove cloth the most tightly of them all, always endeavoring to deliver the high quality the British demanded. Her aunts and cousins worked less diligently. Valli *Periamma* dropped every fourth line. Her cousin Selvi layered in missteps every third cloth she wove. Another cousin used differently weighted threads for warp and weft when she felt rebellious. All those cloths got sorted into the pile meant for local customers.

All those cloths held a message without words—one of refusal. They would not be ruled by strangers any longer.

Thama's fingers trailed over the edge of another length of woven cloth. She thought of the khadi cloth bundles that left their compound in secret, packed in brown paper and twine, traveling across villages. They carried more than fabric. They carried defiance.

An idea came suddenly, like a knot pulling tight in her mind, unformed but insistent. "Salt," she murmured. "My mother talked about salt."

"Salt," her grandmother said even as she kept working, "is what they taxed to keep us hungry. Salt, which every human needs, became a weapon in their hands. But we took it back."

The British tax, she explained, let them control who could produce and sell salt—even in the south, where the heat stole it from their bodies faster than food could restore it. The Raj made gathering salt a crime—villagers could be arrested for harvesting it from beaches or salt pans.

"The Mahatma and seventy-nine of his followers walked from his ashram to the coastal town of Dandi, covering over two hundred miles, in protest. That march showed us, showed the world, that even the smallest thing, gathered from the shore, can shame an empire. And his words echoed everywhere: *Next to air and water, salt is perhaps the greatest necessity of life. It is the only condiment of the poor. In taking this tax, the British rob the people of a God-given right. With this march, I am shaking the foundations of the British Empire.*"

No wonder people still talked about a march that'd happened a decade ago like it was a call to action. The British had thrown Gandhi-ji in jail—again—in the vain hope it would stop more acts of civil disobedience. The weaving community had suffered hard under the tax. Salt was essential to their hand-work, used for cleaning yarn and setting dye. With profits already diminished against mill-made British imports, the tax literally starved their bodies of nutrients and their work of its lifeblood.

Thama stared at the cotton bundles stacked nearby. "Salt speaks," she murmured.

Her grandmother nodded. "It always has." She reached for a shallow bowl of salted water, dipped her fingers in, and rubbed them over the length of spun thread. "Watch. See how the thread stiffens? It absorbs dye better like this. But if you feel it —" She ran the thread between her fingers. "—you can truly understand what the salt has to say."

Thama took the stiffened thread from her grandmother's fingers and laid it gently across her palm. The difference was so slight. You wouldn't see it unless you were searching, but her skin felt it—a ghost of resistance in the fiber. A tightness. A tension. A refusal to lie smooth.

Somewhere, her father was hiding behind another name, another life. But she could still send him a message in the language he would understand—not in words, not in ink. In thread.

"Paatti," she said, daring to put words to her nascent plan. "Do you think... could someone *read* a message like this, just by touch?"

Something flashed in her grandmother's dark eyes—warning or encouragement? "If the reader knows the weaver," she said quietly, "then yes."

A thrill ran through Thama's spine. Her father always said she used too much tension on the warp beam, that her cloth felt too dense, too tight. She could use her weakness as a code. An uneven weave. A few sections tighter than the rest.

To anyone else, it would seem like a child's mistake.

But to her father?

He'd know. He *always* knew her cloth.

She thought of the British soldier who'd torn her mother's cloth last year—called it inferior and unusable. She thought of Gandhi-ji's feet bleeding as he walked toward the sea. And she thought of her father, wrapped in someone else's name, alone in a house not his own.

Not a chapati. And not just a shawl. A ripple. Something small enough to reach him where bigger messages failed. The looms clicked and clacked around her, singing the only song their family had ever known.

And for the first time that day, Thama truly heard it.

Later that evening, as Thama's family retired for the night and the relief shift of workers began, she swept up detritus littering the courtyard. Nearby, her grandmother lit the small lamp near the loom and set out her nighttime offerings: a small bowl of rice, a splash of milk, a line of salt across the threshold. For protection. For strength.

"I saw a boy once," the older woman murmured, so softly Thama could barely hear. "He brought a newspaper to the postmaster. It looked like any other, but the man held it over a lantern. Then words appeared—not from ink, but from lemon juice."

Thama turned sharply. "Did the postmaster read it?"

"He burned it." Her voice was flat. But Thama knew her

grandmother was trying to tell her something bigger. It took her most of the night to figure it out.

Her message would not be written—it would be *felt*—but the British would be watching all the same. She needed to give them something to look for.

She carried an armful of freshly woven cloth to a quiet corner. Unraveling one bolt, she pulled free a length of white thread and dipped it into the salt bowl, setting it beside an untreated piece. In the low light, it gleamed faintly. She cut off a small length and dipped it into the salt bowl. Within minutes, it curled faintly at the edges.

She took a few more strands, dipped just parts of them this time, twisting and pinching them into different states—some more saturated, some barely touched. One thread snapped under the pressure. Another held firm.

Just like her grandmother had instructed, the texture changed depending on how much salt she used.

She laid the samples out beside each other on a wooden board and ran her fingertips over them. A pattern began to form —not of color, but of feel. Slight ridges. Firm against loose. Raised threads like dots and dashes. Pauses. Emphasis.

She didn't know yet what words to encode. Just that they had to say: *Come home. We need you.*

No—not even that. Something smaller. Plainer. Quieter.

Returning to her loom, she smoothed out the threads she'd left behind. The warp was already taut, but she reset the weft to account for the pattern she'd mapped out in her mind.

It was harder than she thought it would be. Controlling tension across even short lines took a level of precision she hadn't yet mastered. Her fingers trembled as she pulled threads tighter in some sections, looser in others, using the salted ones where she needed the fibers to stand out. Each letter had to be guessed at, shaped from feel alone—*H* as a cluster of stiff intersections, *O* as a looser curve.

She didn't need each letter to be perfect—just the rhythm. H became a cluster of stiff intersections, O a loose, open curl. Her father would feel it, like breath across reeds.

House of Salt.

That's all it would say. But it had to be enough.

More than once she had to undo her work and start again. One row buckled where she'd pulled too hard. Another sagged when the salt hadn't dried fully. But slowly, the pattern began to emerge —not visibly, but in the way the cloth felt under her fingers.

Rough. Uneven. Wrong.

It was the worst weaving she'd ever done.

She smiled.

By dawn, her back ached and her eyes burned. But the shawl was finished.

She folded it gently and placed it atop the smooth wrapping paper her grandmother had saved from a sari delivery last week. Then she reached for the newspaper.

Thama dipped a clean reed in a bowl of lemon juice and wrote the decoy message, slowly and carefully, across the inner fold:

Two moons past the last full tide. The jackal waits at the banyan, where the lotus has bloomed. Tell the keeper: the salt is heavy.

She watched the message vanish as the juice dried, leaving nothing but clean newsprint behind.

Wrapping the shawl in the paper, she tied it with a thin rope of leftover cotton. Her fingers trembled again—this time not from effort, but from fear.

If the British read the message and believed it, they might never look further.

But if they didn't—

She pressed the bundle to her chest and whispered a silent prayer. Not to a god, but to the strength in her hands. The same strength that once wove her father's finest *dhoti*. The same strength he'd taught her.

Her mother stirred in the inner room. A rooster called in the distance—still hours before dawn.

She tucked the bundle beneath her shawl and stepped into the dark. Outside, the looms had gone quiet. But not the cloth. Not yet.

The post office squatted like a wounded animal at the edge of the market square, its sandstone walls blistered by heat and posters peeling at the corners. Inside, it was worse—flies buzzed above a stack of telegram slips, the air was thick with sweat and dust, and a soldier leaned against the doorframe, smoking with bored disdain.

Thama clutched her package to her chest and stepped inside. Behind the desk, Sekhar—the thin, bespectacled clerk—glanced up, his nerves twitching beneath his glasses. He smoothed this pencil-line mustache with lanky fingers.

"You have a delivery?" His question was straightforward and expected, the low query hidden underneath less so.

She stepped forward, and giving him an encouraging smile, nodded.

As Sekhar reached for the package, a bark of boots echoed down the corridor.

"Don't touch that," came a voice, crisp and sharp.

Major William J. Prescott strode into the room, his khaki uniform sweat-stained but immaculate in cut, a polished riding crop tucked under one arm like a prop he didn't quite need but liked to show.

He looked Thama over. She imagined what he saw: Brown skin. Thin wrists. Rough cotton sari.

She saw his disdainful judgment: She was poor.

"What do we have here?" he asked. "Another parcel from the rebels?"

Thama said nothing.

Prescott took the package from Sekhar with theatrical slowness. "What's inside?"

"A gift," Thama said in her thick English. "For my father. He works in the city."

Prescott frowned at the wrapping paper. "Sloppy job." He picked at the string. "And where, precisely, does your dear father work?"

Thama swallowed, making a show of being nervous. "He's a khansama, sir. A house steward."

Prescott cocked his head. "And this khansama of yours... does he serve tea or trouble?"

He tapped the side of the paper and held it up to the lantern on the wall. As the heat warmed the page, pale letters began to bloom—slowly, like bruises rising through skin.

Two moons past the last full tide... The jackal waits... Tell the keeper: the salt is heavy.

Prescott read the words aloud, then laughed—a quick, barking sound that turned the room colder.

"Tell me, girl," he said, turning back to Thama. "Is your father the jackal? Are you the lotus?"

"No!" She looked at him with wide eyes. "It's just newspaper—I didn't even know something could be written within it. It's the only wrapping I could find to keep the shawl clean. Please, my father likes homespun cloth—"

Prescott didn't look convinced. "And where exactly did you *find* this wrapping?"

She had anticipated this question. "Someone leaves paper for the goats sometime." She rattled off a location infested with rodents and sewage. "I took the cleanest piece I could find for my gift."

"Gift?" Prescott snorted. "This?" He unwrapped the bundle, revealing the dull cotton inside. He ran his fingers across it once, sneered, and dropped it to the ground.

"Overworked. Coarse. A mess." He looked her dead in the eyes. "You waste our paper, our time, and our soldiers' patience with your filthy scraps."

Thama dropped to her knees and gathered the cloth. She didn't know if she trembled for the performance—or from the real fear that this man might destroy the only chance she had of reaching her father. "Please—I spent so long on this."

Prescott raised his riding crop, pointed it lazily toward the shawl. "Fools sending rags. You people never learn."

Then he turned away, already speaking to a man behind him. "Bring me the last week's logs. We'll see if this jackal girl has sent messages before."

The cloth—her cloth—lay crumpled in the pile beside the waste basket, half-covered by old ledgers and string.

Thama stared at it, breath held. The message—*House of Salt* —was there, but no one saw it. No one felt it.

No one *but her*.

She blinked hard, forcing down the tears that threatened to betray her. She stood slowly, brushed off her hands, and turned to leave.

Behind the desk, Sekhar's eyes followed her—not pitying, but alert. And when she passed by, he reached for a different bundle, shifting a few papers to cover the discarded cloth.

Just enough.

The room felt cavernous and thin, like it was stretching away from her.

Behind the desk, Sekhar cleared his throat gently. "You may go," he said.

Thama bowed her head, murmured a thank-you she barely meant, and turned to leave.

As she passed the pile one last time, her eyes flicked toward the shawl. Its salted edges curled faintly in the lamplight—ugly and uneven. Unread. But still there. Still waiting to be felt.

She walked out. And watched from across the street.

A breath later, Sekhar rose. He waited until the hallway was quiet and Prescott's footsteps had faded, then stepped around the desk. He shuffled a few ledgers, stacked some string-bound envelopes, and slipped the shawl underneath them—just enough to tuck it back into the outgoing dispatch tray.

He didn't say a word. But he met her eyes and gave a quiet nod.

Elsewhere, in a cooler room behind shuttered windows, Major Prescott sat at a long wooden desk stacked with maps and surveillance reports. A lantern hissed quietly beside him. He reread the lemon-juice message now under warm glass.

Two moons past the last full tide. The jackal waits at the banyan... Tell the keeper: the salt is heavy.

He scowled, irritated at having to spend his precious time on this dimwit girl and her flea-ridden cloth. Still, someone had written this message and left it for someone else to pass on.

No such date lined up with known insurgent activity. No jackal. No banyan of interest. The poetic phrasing read more like a schoolgirl's fable than encrypted instruction. It looked like nonsense. But nonsense could be cover.

He circled a phrase with a pencil. *The salt is heavy.*

A taunt? Or a challenge he wasn't clever enough to crack? He hated riddles. He hated the thought of being outwitted by a servant or a slip of a girl.

He tapped the paper with the blunt end of his pen. Something itched at the back of his mind.

That address—where the package was meant to go. A servant's quarters in R.S. Puram. That district had been under scrutiny before. An official had once reported suspicious kitchen staff—names that didn't match the census, documents that came late.

He pulled the slip toward him and wrote:

Revisit address. Possible courier.

He paused, then added:

Question servants—esp. "Velu." Check aliases.

He looked up, frowning. Something still didn't feel right. The girl had been too frightened to fake the fear. Yet the message —this lemon-ink riddling—was *meaningless.* A red herring.

His eyes darted toward the trash pile from earlier.

But it was gone.

He stood, walked over, sifted through some crumpled papers. The dirty shawl. The one he'd mocked. It wasn't there.

Prescott narrowed his eyes.

"Find out who touched the outgoing dispatch," he barked into the empty hallway. "Double-check the manifests."

But even as he said it, he knew it would be too late. The cloth was gone. A message, if there ever was one, had moved on.

Deep in the city, the delivery came late in the day, slipped between a box of canned goods from Calcutta and a stack of English newspapers smelling faintly of sea. A quiet thing, easy to miss.

Velu—known to no one here as Arunachalam—was setting out the evening tea tray when a manservant called his name. "Post for you."

He wiped his hands and stepped into the side hall where packages were left for the staff. A single bundle sat atop a wooden bench, wrapped in brown paper and tied with worn cotton string. No letter. No note.

He unwrapped the odd package and pulled out a shawl. His hands told him an essential truth before his eyes could.

The weave was wrong.

Coarse. Clumsy. Too tight in some places, loose in others. This wasn't the work of a child, but of someone trying *not* to be precise.

He unfolded it slowly. A homespun shawl fell into his hands, stiffened in places with salt. The scent hit him faintly, like sea air in a dry courtyard—distant, but unmistakable.

Arunachalam spread the cloth across the table. His hands moved without thinking, tracing the raised threads the way a weaver tests for strength.

There. A rhythm. He closed his eyes.

H. O. U. S. E.

Each stiffened cluster of threads formed a shape he knew.

O. F.

The tension in the fibers told him more than words ever could.

S. A. L. T.

His eyes opened. The breath he took felt sharper than usual. *House of Salt.*

He glanced toward the window. Outside, the British officer

he served—Major Woodhouse—shouted instructions at a gardener, his voice thick with gin and condescension.

Velu's hand tightened on the edge of the table.

He had been patient—watching, listening, gathering names and routes. And now his daughter had sent the message he had been waiting for—through thread, not ink. Through labor, not letters. Because there was no weave she could make that he wouldn't recognize.

He folded the shawl carefully, reverently. No tears came, but something in his chest ached with pride.

He tucked the cloth under his tunic. There was still a meal to serve.

But not many more.

As he carried the tea tray into the sitting room, he paused by the threshold, watching the officer slumped in his chair, demanding cardamom without saying please.

Velu set the tray down. "I will be there, Thama."

Not a statement, but a vow.

The British never found the cloth. But a train car derailed two weeks later, and the telegraph wires near R.S. Puram fell silent for three nights.

A ripple, passed hand to hand. Still moving. Still resisting.

Author's Note

Mohandas Karamchand Gandhi, later known as The Mahatma or Venerable One, was an Indian lawyer who spent much of his life working to expel colonial rule of India through non-violent means. In August 1942, Gandhi launched the Quit India Movement, igniting mass civil disobedience and protests across the country. Acts of rebellion such as railway sabotage, factory and mill strikes, telegraph and power line cuts, and shipyard disruptions were widespread yet often unpredictable and localized. Over time these uprisings intensified and expanded, adding to the growing pressure that ultimately forced the British to concede India's independence.

BIOGRAPHIES

Ana Brazil's novels and short stories feature bodacious women who resolve their problems in their own special way. Reach Ana at anabrazil.com.

C.V. Lee writes award-winning fiction about forgotten heroes and heroines of the past. Find her at cvlee.com.

Linda Ulleseit's novels are the stories of women in her family who were extraordinary but unsung. Find her at ulleseit.com.

Anne M. Beggs is a writing, riding grandma. Her Dahlquin Series is a family saga set in Medieval Ireland, a volatile island always poised for civil war or invasion. Please join her at annembeggs.com.

Kathryn Pritchett usually writes about strong women forged in the American West, so writing about Paul Cezanne was an "artful" departure for her. Connect with her at thingselemental.com or on instagram @klooslip.

Edie Cay writes award-winning historical romance about intrepid people who defy the odds. Find her at ediecay.com.

Jonathan Posner writes action adventure stories set in the 16th century. Find out more at jonathanposnerauthor.com.

Alina Rubin writes adventurous historical fiction featuring heroines with strong voices and able hands. Find her at alinarubinauthor.com.

Vanitha Sankaran writes lush fiction rooted in myths, beliefs, and culture, following fictional people as they navigate historical times. Find her at vanithasankaran.com.

ABOUT PAPER LANTERN WRITERS

The Paper Lantern Writers are an author collective focused on historical fiction of all eras. From Medieval Europe to Gilded Age America (and beyond), our books will take you on the journeys of a lifetime.

PAPER LANTERN
WRITERS

Find us at www.paperlanternwriters.com

facebook.com/paperlanternwriters

instagram.com/paperlanternwriters

youtube.com/@paperlanternwriters

ALSO BY PAPER LANTERN WRITERS

Fiction

Unlocked

Beneath a Midwinter Moon

Destiny Comes Due

Echoes of Small Things

Non-Fiction

Crafting Stories from the Past: A How-To Guide for Writing
Historical Fiction

www.paperlanternwriters.com

www.ingramcontent.com/pod-product-compliance
Lightning Source LLC
Chambersburg PA
CBHW060638260626
47161CB00008B/2909